THE LAST GOODBYE

THE BEGINNING

BERNADETTE MARIE

5 PRINCE PUBLISHING

Published by 5 PRINCE PUBLISHING & BOOKS, LLC

PO Box 865, Arvada, CO 80001

www.5PrinceBooks.com

ISBN digital: 978-1-63112-232-3

ISBN print: 978-1-63112-233-0

Cover Credit: Marianne Nowicki, Bernadette Soehner

Finding Hope

THE THREE MRS. MONROES TRILOGY

Amelia

Penelope

Vivian

THE ASPEN CREEK SERIES

First Kiss

Unexpected Admirer

On Thin Ice

Indomitable Spirit

THE DENVER BRIDE SERIES

Cart Before the Horse

Never Saw it Coming

Candy Kisses

ROMANTIC SUSPENSE by BERNADETTE MARIE

Chasing Shadows

PARANORMAL ROMANCE by BERNADETTE MARIE

The Tea Shop

The Last Goodbye

To Stan,
In this case,
Forever and a Day
is only
The Beginning

Daddy,
I miss you every minute of every day.
Thank you for all of the lessons you taught me.
I can hear all of your words of wisdom,
even from heaven.
I love you!

ACKNOWLEDGMENTS

Mommy and Sissy - I hope that this book might bring you some peace as it did me. It's been a long year, but we can still hear him.

My Boys - Always remember the good things. Wisdom comes in those little phrases you catch yourself saying.

Clare, Jeannie, Lisa V., Chris, Leslie, Stephanie, Corinne, Lisa M., Shannon, Cate, and Sue (I'm probably missing a bunch of you) Thank You, from the bottom of my heart for making the transition of this year easier. Your love and compassion continues to carry me.

My Readers - Thank you for reading my stories!

LETTER TO THE READER

The Last Goodbye has been a story that has been brewing for years. When my paternal grandmother passed away, and we were spending time in the mortuary, I thought it was such an interesting place to set a story. As the staff worked with us on arrangements, I knew I needed to incorporate that into my books. Years passed, and the story was fresh again when my maternal grandmother passed, but the story wasn't ready to be written. In June of 2018 I lost my father. I wasn't ready for that—none of us were. But again I was spending time with people who helped to bring us comfort, and the story was ready to be written. This book took longer than most for me to write, but the journey to bring it to the page was worth it. Feeling the connection from this realm to the other, and *knowing* that we can hear them and they can hear us, brought me comfort. I have fallen in love with writing paranormal romances, and perhaps visiting those who have left us physically is the reason behind that. And much like Grace, in the story, I think this is fitting for a last goodbye—but just as in the story, it's only the beginning.

Thank you for reading my stories!
Bernadette Marie

THE LAST GOODBYE

CHAPTER 1

*D*etails were important when it came to the life of a loved one who had passed. Grace Carter could almost hear her grandmother's voice repeat those very words as she explained the family business to her when she was a young girl.

"We give a family the last memory. Every detail has to be just right," she would say before she went into the room which Grace was not allowed in until she was much older.

Now, as she read through the file for Mrs. Nora Campbell, she thought about what her grandmother taught her.

Mrs. Nora Campbell was preceded in death by her husband George nearly ten years earlier. Grace gave thought to where she would have been when George Campbell died. The Carter family had taken care of his arrangements and prepared him for burial. In fact, it had been her father who had tended to Mr. Campbell when he'd passed.

Ten years ago, she would have been studying cosmetology on the living. The thought caused her to chuckle to herself as she sat alone in one of the rooms where they would go over arrangements with the families of the deceased.

The Carter Mortuary had been in her family for nearly one hundred and fifty years. Of course, she'd been teased ruthlessly as a child about spending time with dead bodies, but she knew it was an essential part of life—the end of it. It wasn't all about dead bodies. There was so much more to it.

Grace read through the obituary that the family had penned for Nora and looked over some of the items that they asked for on the paperwork. Usually, there was a photo of the beloved, one that she would use to create the lasting image the family would take with them after seeing her for the last time. And it was the reason she was sitting alone in the room, her earbuds plugged into her ears with her movie sound-track playlist blaring, waiting for the grandson to arrive with the photo that was missing from Nora's file.

She loved her work and took great pride in what she did. It didn't hurt any that the deceased could talk to her, but she didn't much care for that aspect of her job. It was a gift inherited from her grandmother. If her father had it, she'd never been told, though she suspected he had some kind of gift. Grace supposed it was good that she didn't see the spirit too but only heard them. Thus, the headphones were always plugged in when she worked.

For a moment, she closed her eyes when the theme song from the movie Up began. Oh, what a movie. Only Disney could make you cry for the first ten minutes of a movie just by showing the backstory of a romance that would forever stand the test of time. Even sitting alone in the room, she could feel herself tear up just thinking about it.

But her thought was shattered when a hand tapped her shoulder sending her up and out of the chair, the file on Nora Campbell scattering across the room.

With her eyes wide open now, she pulled out the earbuds and stared into the crystal blue, apologetic eyes, of a man who had his hands up in defense.

"I am so sorry. I didn't mean to startle you like that," he said with his voice cracking. "I was told I could find Grace Carter here. I thought you might be her. Again, I didn't mean to…"

"You're fine. I'm fine." She pressed her hand to her heart that pounded like a bass drum. "I just zoned out. I didn't hear you come in." Taking a long deep breath, she steadied herself. "I'm Grace Carter," she offered as she held out her hand to the man.

"Matthew Campbell. Nora Campbell's grandson."

With his hand grasped in hers, she rested her other hand atop his. "My condolences on your grandmother."

"Thank you," he said as she let go of his hand. "My mother had sent me home for a photo of her and to get her handkerchief too. She always had a handkerchief in her sleeve. We just thought it would be nice to have that added too."

"Of course." She held her hand out to take the items he offered to her. "I'll be working with her this afternoon, and I'll take care with her. You have my word. She will look like the grandmother you always remembered so that your memories of her are pleasant ones."

"I appreciate that. Everyone has been so pleasant. It's making the process much easier." He ran his hand over his chestnut hair. "I know that when someone is ninety, and they die it shouldn't be so hard. You expect them to die."

"Death is never easy, no matter the age of the loved one. We have a lot of resources if you find

BERNADETTE MARIE

that you need them to help with the grieving process."

Matthew let out a chuckle as he dropped his hand. "I know I'll be fine. I was very close to my grandmother. She'll be missed."

"That's very sweet."

"Is my family still in the room?" he asked, and Grace gave it some thought.

"No. They all headed out to the cemetery to confirm her final resting place."

"Ah, in other words, they left me."

Grace smiled. "If you would give me a moment to secure these items, I'd be happy to take you out there."

"I'd appreciate that."

She turned to gather the papers she'd dropped on the floor and nearly knocked heads with Matthew as he knelt down to help her.

They shared a laugh as they avoided the collision.

"I'll bet you deal with all kinds of people," he mused as he helped gather the papers. "Some are distraught, and others are clumsy like me."

"You're right, I see all kinds. I don't think you're clumsy at all. Thank you for your help," she said as they both stood. "I'll be just a moment if you want to meet me at the reception desk."

He gazed at her for another moment with those dreamy blue eyes and then turned and walked out of the room.

Grace gathered her composure before following him and heading to the back where she would leave the items she'd collected. However, she couldn't help but turn to take one more glance at the grandson who loved his grandmother. Nora Campbell had some good genes. Her grandson was nice to look at.

4

CHAPTER 2

*M*atthew watched the video on the large TV screen behind the reception desk. The slide show showed a photo of a person who's funeral or memorial was planned. The images captivated him. Then the stark reality hit him that his grandmother's photo would soon be displayed because she too had passed and would have a funeral.

He wiped away the bead of sweat that had formed on his brow. Thirty-five-year-olds shouldn't be shaken by the death of their grandmother. How many people got to say they had a grandmother still living when they were in their mid-thirties? Matthew acknowledged just how lucky he'd been.

Grandma Nora had been a considerable influence in his life. She was the one who had made him consider being a reporter. A smile formed on his lips as he thought of the days she'd play with him while his mother worked. He would wear one of his grandfather's hats with a homemade press pass stuck in the band. With a small golf pencil, he would take down notes from the witness—his ever-entertaining grandmother. When he had everything he needed for a story, she would pull out the old Underwood typewriter that she kept in the closet that had belonged to her mother, and she'd let him write his story. When his grandfather would return from work, as well as his mother, they'd each get a copy of that day's news.

God, he was going to miss her.

The photo his mother had chosen of her, which he'd brought back to the mortuary and no doubt it would be the one they displayed on the TV screen, depicted his grandmother the way he'd always remember her.

Her hair was white, and her wise blue eyes gazed lovingly from behind tri-focal glasses. Pink painted lips turned up into the smile that always greeted him. The dress she wore in the photo was the one she'd chosen to be buried in, and he thought that suited her just fine.

There had never been a day when his grandma Nora hadn't worn a bumblebee pin on her blouse or jacket. She always reminded him that the bumblebee shouldn't be able to fly, they're not made for it. But they did fly, and he could fly too as long as he believed he could.

As a family, they had all decided that she would need a bumble bee pin attached to her dress. However, they also agreed that they should get a new one that wasn't very expensive. The one she'd always worn was a custom-made piece his grandfather had commissioned. In time, someone would get the pin that she'd always cherished. She'd always said when the time was right for someone to have it, the family would know.

Matthew wasn't sure how that would work. How were they supposed to know? He assumed his father and his sisters would decide. No doubt it would go to someone on his aunt's side of the family. He most certainly could say he didn't want the pin to wear.

"Thanks for being patient," Grace said to him snapping him from his thoughts. "I'll take you out to the site now."

"I appreciate that."

She led the way from the mortuary to the parking lot where an upscale golf cart awaited. Grace motioned for him to get in, and so he did.

"Not what I was expecting," he admitted as he watched as she gracefully climbed into the cart.

"We find that it's the easiest way to get around. My father would have taken your family out in one of our larger family cars."

She put the cart into drive and started out of the lot.

"Your father was the man working on the arrangements?"

"Yes. He and my mother tend to most of the arrangements. But my father will also help with preparation as well."

He knew preparation was the PC word for what they really did. Matthew was a reporter after all—a seeker of knowledge. He knew what it took to *prepare* a body, but he wasn't going to even imagine that they were going to do that to his grandmother. Nora Campbell wasn't practical enough to be cremated, well in his opinion. Matthew didn't understand the need to be embalmed and dressed up only to be closed up and buried in the ground. But his grandmother, though sweet, sincere, and gentle was also very vain. Hence the reason her lips were always glossed pink.

She would have had it no other way than to have her exquisitely preserved body on display.

The thought made him chuckle, and he noticed Grace shift him a look. "Sorry. Just had a funny thought," he admitted. "How long have you been doing this?"

She gave him a little shrug as she gently turned a corner into the cemetery. "I've been taking part in everything since I was a young girl. I used to fold the programs and vacuum the chapel. Then I moved up to setting up the floral arrangements that were delivered. In time I worked the front desk, I've sat in on arrangements a few times, but when I decided I really wanted to be a cosmetologist, I left and did that for a few years However, there is a pull to the work I do, and I eventually came back to work the family business."

He considered his next words carefully. "Family businesses don't usually deal with dead bodies."

She let out a little laugh as she turned the cart again down another well-groomed road lined with rows and rows of headstones.

"Every family business is different I'm sure. I don't know if I'd sell cars if my family owned a car lot. But I do know that it's an awesome responsibility to make your loved one look the way you remember them, and that is your lasting memory of them—at peace."

Matthew let out a defeated breath. "You certainly have a way with comforting words."

"Thank you," she said as she waved at two men who had set up lawn chairs between two headstones. He was quite sure he also heard the sounds of a baseball game.

Cranking his head, he continued to watch the men, each with a beer in their hand and a smile on their mouths as they carried on in a conversation.

"Mr. Leeds and Mr. Rodriguez," she offered, and he turned his attention back to Grace. "They're wives were laid to rest only a few days apart. They met while they visited, and they became friends. They meet out here each day there is a baseball game. They listen to the game and have a beer together with their wives."

Matthew had to turn his head and steady himself. He thought that might just have been the sweetest thing he'd ever heard in his life.

"We have a few other families that hold, well we call them block parties, here in the cemetery. They've all gotten to know each other through circumstance."

"You know," he began and then cleared the emotion from his throat, "I might have to do a story on that."

"A story?"

"I'm a reporter."

"On TV?"

"Yes, by chance. With less circulation in newspaper, I made the jump a year ago and luckily had a friend at channel four that could get me a job. I do the pieces on people in the community, not so much of the hardcore news anymore."

Grace let out a sigh as she slowed when they came upon the family car, and he saw his family amongst the headstones.

"I think those pieces about people are so necessary. The world needs good news."

He'd gotten complacent about that he decided as she parked the cart behind the car. "You're right. Do you think Mr. Leeds and Mr. Rodriguez would talk to me?"

She smiled, and he found that it twisted him up. "If you'll leave me a business card or your email at the front desk, I'll be sure to ask them."

"I'd appreciate that," he said realizing it was time for him to join his family. "Thank you for bringing me out here."

"My pleasure. I'll talk to you on Friday."

He almost had to ask her why, but then remembered, as he heard his mother call his name, that he'd see her at the funeral.

Matthew gave Grace a small wave and walked back toward his family. Who knew that a day he'd dreaded would turn out to not be so bad?

CHAPTER 3

*G*race's father had given her a wave as she pulled away after having dropped off Matthew. She waved again at Mr. Leeds and Mr. Rodriguez on her drive back to the mortuary where she would begin her work on Nora Campbell.

She should have taken a moment to ask Matthew who his grandmother really was. What did she like? What did she do? What were her hobbies?

The more she knew about a person, the easier it was to make them appear at rest. Oh, she could ask her herself, but she tried not to do that. She didn't mind that her grandmother passed on her gift of talking to the deceased, but Grace would rather do her job without the interruptions.

As she parked the cart and walked into the mortuary, she listened as Ella Walsh, their receptionist of nearly forty years, greeted and calmed a family who had arrived. The grandmother, with her black purse in the crook of her arm, sobbed. A woman held an arm around her consoling her, but she too cried. The man spoke to Ella, who offered a box of tissues to the woman. Death came in many forms. To some, it was expected. To others it was a painful ordeal—and that was for the living.

Grace offered a consoling smile to the man as she passed walking to the back of the mortuary and through the two large mahogany doors to the room where Nora Campbell waited for her.

She gathered the papers she'd had before Matthew had returned with the photo, which now sat on top of the stack. Juan, one of their morticians, said hello as he passed her in the hallway, and she laughed as he made a peace-out sign with his fingers. It was a falsehood if anyone thought those who worked with the dead didn't live happy lives.

As she looked down at the photo of Nora Campbell, she turned the knob on the door and pushed it open. With happiness still clouding her brain from the chat with Matthew and the antics of Juan, she closed the door behind her.

Nora Campbell rested on the table for her. She'd been cleaned and prepped by Juan when he'd finished with her. It was her opinion, but she always thought the elderly looked more peaceful in death than younger people did. Perhaps they'd happily fulfilled their lives.

"So, what did you think of him?" A voice filled Grace's ears, and she cringed as she touched her ears in search for her headphones, only to find she'd never put them on.

Letting out a long, slow sigh, she approached Nora.

"Think of who?" she asked as she looked down at the pale face of the woman Matthew called his grandmother, who remained motionless, her eyes and mouth still closed.

"My grandson. What did you think?"

Grace often wondered if her *gift* would be easier

to deal with if she could see the person's spirit standing in the corner of the room. But it didn't work that way. All she could do was hear their voices, and death was always in the room.

Luckily, she didn't hear anyone if their bodies weren't with her. The cemetery didn't bother her, and neither did morgues when the bodies were all closed away. It was only when she was working one on one with a person that they could talk to her, and it was why she wore her headphones so she couldn't hear them.

"Matthew is a fascinating man," Grace said as she turned to reach for the photo of Nora. "Do you prefer rose pink or a deeper red pink for your lips?" she asked, because why not ask if they were having a conversation.

"Oh, I do love a rose pink," Nora told her. "My grandson is single," she offered, and Grace heard her laugh.

It brought a smile to Grace's lips as she searched her pallet of colors for the perfect rose pink to use when she got to that part of Nora's makeup.

"I don't believe that," Grace humored aloud though the voice she heard was only in her head. "He's an attractive man who is very kind. I would think he has women lined up."

"You would think so," she agreed as Grace began to apply the makeup that would bring peace to Nora Campbell's family when they looked at her. "He works too hard."

"I can understand that."

"You work too hard too. I can tell that about you." Nora's tone carried a warning.

"My schedule is dictated by the events of something, or someone, greater than me."

"Even God took a day to rest," Nora reminded her

and Grace thought she saw the woman's face smile, but after a few blinks, she knew she'd imagined that.

This wasn't the first in-depth conversation Grace had had with the deceased. Mrs. Rodriguez was a talker when she'd been on Grace's table. That was the day her brother had stepped on her earphones and crushed them under his *after the holiday weight*, as he'd reminded her when she'd come unglued.

Mrs. Rodriguez had had a lot to say, probably because she'd had a lot of life left to live, and she hadn't had a moment to finish her business on the earth. Cancer had taken her at a young fifty-two. Grace still kept the list she'd written down; which Mrs. Rodriguez had insisted she write. She just wasn't sure what she was ever supposed to do with it.

Because she knew she'd sound crazy, Grace had never shared the list or the conversation with Mr. Rodriguez, even though she spoke to him weekly. No, until she knew what she could do with it, she kept the list tucked away in a book in her desk. Along with the list, she kept the combination to a private safe that Mr. Jackson had told her about six years ago. She soon realized that her job would continue to put her in the line of fire for chatty spirits if she didn't wear her earphones and block them out, and she'd worn them religiously ever since.

Grace gently applied a foundation to Nora Campbell's face that would give her a healthy glow. She couldn't help but be a little cynical about the whole process, but the dead had been prepared for centuries so that they looked good when they arrived in heaven, and the living remembered them as they were in life and not in death.

"Matthew is a reporter," Nora continued as Grace applied her makeup.

"He told me."

"He's a good one too."

"I have no doubt. He said you were the one that got him interested in it."

She heard the sigh, and again was sure she saw a smile, but it was only in the sounds, not on the body. "We used to play newspaper when he'd stay at my house. I never thought he'd become a newsman on TV. But he has the face for it."

Grace would agree. "Done well, it's an admirable career."

"Of course. You should have dinner with him," Nora stated, and Grace dropped the brush she'd been using.

"I don't see that happening. He's in mourning right now."

"Oh, hell. He'll get over it. I'm old. I was supposed to die."

Grace was grateful to have someone who understood the process, the younger spirits didn't always have the same attitude.

"Not many people want to date a woman who sits with the deceased all day," Grace informed her as she brushed the pink that Nora had chosen on her lips. "Most people find this creepy."

"I find it as admirable as Matthew's job. The world is filled with hate and crime. He reports it with compassion. You take great consideration into also giving compassion to those left behind. I'm not naive to think that all of your customers are old ladies who were ready to die. There are children that die. Horrible accidents happen, and people like you make the living see the deceased as they were, not as they died. Admirable," she stated again. "You two would have a lot to talk about."

Grace felt the tears sting her throat as she blended blush on Nora's cheeks. "Thank you for appreciating what I do." She sat back. "How do you look?"

"Dead," Nora said with a laugh that had Grace joining her. "I think this will bring them all comfort. Now," she cleared her throat, "if you'd like to bring me comfort in eternity, you'll have dinner with my grandson."

Grace let her shoulders drop. "If I tell him you told me to ask him to dinner, he will think I'm crazy and run out."

"You don't give him enough credit. You can tell him about our conversation. And you know what? If he does run out, then he's not the man I thought he was."

Grace gathered her things and took one more look at Nora Campbell. "You are inspiring. I have another lady that I need to attend to now. I will see you when your family comes to visit."

"I will talk to you then," Nora said, and then Grace could feel her drift away, as the spirits often did when they were done speaking.

As she walked through the door and closed it, she leaned up against it. Seriously, the woman had nothing better to do in the afterlife than to tell Grace to ask her grandson out. Was he that bad of a case that she worried he'd never date? Grace's mother always did tell her she was too hard on herself. Why was it too hard to believe that a nice deceased woman wanted her to simply have dinner with her grandson?

"Mrs. Harper is ready for you," Juan said as he closed the door to the room across the hall.

"I'll be right in. Mrs. Campbell is ready for placement."

Juan gave her a nod. "I'll let Chase know."

CHAPTER 4

Matthew wondered what his grandmother would think of all the fussing on her behalf. She'd be flattered because she understood the process and knew that ultimately they were all thinking about her. However, he could almost hear her from the beyond telling them to put their money away and spend it on more important matters. She would say to them that there were too many roses, they didn't need to rent a hearse to have her hauled from the church where she was married to her final resting place. And had his mother really called a caterer for a luncheon? Oh, that would have had Grandma Nora up in arms, he thought as he drove home from the cemetery, exhausted from the day.

Pulling up in front of his townhouse, he groaned as his stomach grumbled. He'd had a bagel for breakfast on his way to his parents' house, but that was all he'd eaten. In fact, since they'd had lunch the day before to discuss plans, he didn't think he'd eaten at all. He laughed as he put his car in park and turned off the engine. If it had been someone else that had passed, Grandma Nora would have made sure everyone ate and drank all day. That was the kind of woman she was. Fussing was her trademark, and he was going to miss it.

Tears stung his throat, so he cleared it as he pushed open his door and stepped out onto the sidewalk where he first noticed the pair of pink high heels on long bare legs standing just a few feet away.

Matthew lifted his eyes to see Rebecca Barnes standing there in a dress that matched the color of her shoes. Long blonde curls flowed over her shoulders, and big black sunglasses shielded the blue eyes, which he knew were sad a pitiful behind those lenses.

"Are you doing okay, Matt? I just heard about your grandmother, and I rushed right over," she said, the pitch of her voice piercing his ears.

"I'm fine, Rebecca. Thank you for stopping by."

"Of course, I brought you dinner too," she offered as she turned her head to acknowledge the bag which sat on the steps to his door.

"You didn't have to do that."

"Sure I did. I knew you needed some company, so here I am." Pink lips turned up into a smile, and Matthew felt his stomach drop. This was the last thing he needed tonight, but having known Rebecca Barnes since middle school, he knew damn good and well she wasn't leaving any time soon. He might as well satisfy his growling stomach with whatever she'd carried out from a restaurant for him.

The moment Matthew was out of the car, Rebecca's arm looped through his, and she tugged him toward the front door.

He should have taken his mother's invitation to stay at their house for the night, but he couldn't see any reason to do so since he only lived a half hour across town. Maybe his mother had a psychic episode or something and was giving him an out—and he hadn't listened.

The thought made him chuckle, and Rebecca turned her head to look at him. "I just thought of something funny. It's nothing," he offered to preempt her question.

Taking the key from his pocket, he unlocked the door and pushed it open.

Rebecca picked up the bag and headed inside and right to the kitchen, just as if she lived there.

Matthew tossed his keys on the counter and went to the refrigerator for a beer. "Would you like one?"

"You know I don't drink beer. Don't you have any wine? White?"

Matthew twisted the top from his bottle and nodded. "Sure."

He might as well just look at the opportunity for of company as a gift; otherwise, it was going to be a very long night.

He pulled the wine from the cupboard, as well a glass.

"You don't chill it?" Rebecca looked up at him a bit horrified as she pulled containers out of the bag.

"I don't drink wine too often."

Her lips pursed. "It'll be fine." She pulled out the last container and smiled. "I guess dinner is served. I'll set the table. Why don't you go change? You look like you need to put on something a little more comfortable."

Matthew looked down at his dress shirt, sans tie, and his dark denim. In his world, he was dressed reasonably comfortable. Did she want him to wear sweats and a muscle shirt while she was all gussied up like Reese Witherspoon in Legally Blonde?

"I'll be right down," he conceded as he started up the stairs to his bedroom.

Matthew unbuttoned his shirt and put it into the laundry bag he kept in the corner of his closet. Then he searched for a T-Shirt, settling on a dark blue Denver Bronco one.

With a quick look in the mirror, he decided he looked comfortable enough in his own home—realizing he still had on his shoes, but he wasn't going to go that far. After all, Rebecca was in his house, and that was making him nervous. At this point, he wanted to eat, because he was starving, and get her out. There was no doubt she was just being friendly, but he knew there was interest there, but it was only one-sided. In his current mental state, he certainly didn't want her messing with his emotions.

Just as he walked out of his bedroom, Rebecca started up the stairs. She flashed her smile at him. "I thought maybe you'd fallen asleep. You look so tired."

Hoping to halt her advancement up the stairs, he hurried down them. "Nope. I'm ready to eat."

Sliding by her, he walked back to the kitchen where she'd set his small table with plates and dished out the meal. "Olive Garden?"

"Yes. It was easy to pick up from work. I thought you liked Olive Garden."

"I do. Thanks for thinking of it."

Well, he thought, at least she knew him well enough to feed him one of his favorites. For that, he'd be thankful.

"Are the plans coming together for the funeral?" Rebecca asked as she picked up a breadstick and nibbled the end of it.

"Yes." Matthew picked up a fork and spun it into his spaghetti. "The family that runs the mortuary is very efficient and kind. They're helping us out a lot. I think everything is just as Grandma would have wanted it."

"That is so sweet," she said dabbing her eyes with her napkin.

Seriously, the last thing he needed tonight was Rebecca sobbing over his grandmother.

"Interesting story though," he began as he put the bite in his mouth, chewed, and swallowed. "The woman who is preparing my grandmother drove me out to where she'll be buried, but along the way, there were two men there who sit in their lawn chairs and listen to the baseball game. They've become friends, and they include their wives in their friendship."

Rebecca's eyes had gone wide as she contemplated her forkful of salad. "That's inconsiderate, isn't it? Lawn chairs in the cemetery and listening to the ball game?"

He took another bite humored by her reaction. "She said once in a while they have a beer too. And another area the families have a block party of sorts. It's quite amazing."

She drank down her wine when she'd finished her bite. "It just doesn't seem sacred."

Matthew shrugged. "I was thinking of doing a story about it. I have plans to call the woman who showed me around and see if she can put me in touch with them."

"You're going to publicize such a thing?"

"I don't think it's bad. They're celebrating the memories of their loved ones."

He watched her process the conversation, as he'd watched her do so many times before. Then, just as he'd expected, the smile on her pink lips returned, and her mannerism changed back to giving him her full attention.

What he wouldn't have given for her to do that when they were twelve, and those golden curls had stirred him up in ways he didn't understand, but she didn't notice him then. It wasn't until their senior year when he'd been smitten with another blonde beauty that Rebecca set her eyes on him and never took them off.

She'd been married for a short while—twice, but she always came back seeking friendship, and gratefully he'd only ever given her that. But he had noticed as they'd crossed the line into their thirty-fifth year, she'd been a bit more aggressive in her pursuit of him. There had been a few times, perhaps in his own desperation, that he'd thought of giving into her, but that just hadn't come to fruition yet.

"What are your plans after dinner?" Rebecca asked sitting back and sipping at her wine.

"I'll be heading to bed. I've taken the past three days off, and I'll be off on Friday too. I'll be in the studio early tomorrow editing a piece I did that they're playing in my absence."

"I'm sure the ratings go down when you're not there." She ran her finger over the rim of her glass, no doubt in a seductive move that didn't twist him up as it once might have.

"I don't know about that. They've been very gracious to let me have so much time off to be with my family."

"I could stay with you for a bit if you like. It's always good to have some comfort during these hard times," she offered as Matthew's phone rang and he pulled it from his back pocket.

He didn't recognize the phone number, but he'd be damned if he didn't answer it and hope for some kind of emergency so that he'd have to excuse himself.

"Matthew? This is Grace Carter from..."

"Hey, Grace. How are you?" He said her name aloud with hopes it would resonate with Rebecca.

"I'm well. Thank you. I'm so sorry to bother you at home, and I know it's late."

"Not a problem. What can I do for you?" he asked as he took a breadstick from the bag and watched as Rebecca tried to occupy herself as if she weren't trying to eavesdrop.

"This sounds silly, and it probably could have waited until tomorrow. I have a few questions about your grandmother. The handkerchief you brought to put in her sleeve, which sleeve?"

Matthew bit back the smile and kept his face as sober as he could. "Her right."

"Wonderful. And the bee pin?"

Now he couldn't help but chuckle as well. "Left side, over her heart."

"I appreciate your help. I didn't want to bother your parents, but my father forgot to get that information."

"I'm glad you called. It was nice to talk to you," he said and heard the snap of Rebecca's teeth on her fork. "I'll see you on Friday."

GRACE DISCONNECTED the call and put her phone back into her pocket. She looked down at Nora Campbell with her pink lips and perfectly styled hair.

"Okay, he told me the handkerchief goes under your right sleeve and the pin on your left, over your heart."

The warm laughter that filled her ears made her smile. "I told you he knew everything about me," the voice said as she placed the items on Nora where they belonged. "And was he happy to hear from you?"

"I couldn't say. But he was very polite."

"And if you weren't interested, you wouldn't have come in here to fuss over me, especially since you

don't plan to put that pin on me until my viewing tomorrow night."

Grace sucked in a breath. She'd prepared herself
to see Matthew on Friday at the funeral, but she
hadn't even considered the viewing. Perhaps it was
because she had initially been scheduled to have the
night off. Well, she couldn't really do that now, could
she? That would be letting down Mrs. Campbell.

"I've enjoyed talking to you. That's all," Grace said.
"I'll make sure that everything is perfect for your
family tomorrow."

"I know you will. You're a very thorough woman.
You'll appreciate Matthew. He's thorough as well.
He's very neat and tidy too. I would think women
would appreciate that in a man. My husband was
fine, and I made it my job to always take care of him.
My sons, they were messier as children than as
adults. Matthew, on the other hand, he always liked
things neat and tidy. You have to appreciate that."

Grace thought of her own brother and how even
as a grown man he was a slob. "Again, he seems like a
very nice man. I'll talk to him tomorrow. Is there
anything you would like me to tell him?" she asked
and quickly wished she could retract it.

"Since you asked. They're going to be looking for
the key to my firebox. It's under the mattress in my
bedroom. My roses will need to be cut back. I
promised a bush to Matthew's sister Brittany, so if he
could dig it up and replant it at her house, that would
be lovely. Also, my veil was passed down for generations. You're welcome to wear it for your day," Nora
said as she laughed again and then it faded away,
which signified the end of their conversation.

Grace pressed her fingers to her eyes as she
thought about what Nora had told her. How was she
supposed to convey all of that to Matthew without

sounding like a loon? Oh, and the veil? Nora Campbell didn't really think that just because her grandson was single, and so was Grace, that they'd get married someday, did she?

Grace closed the lid to Nora's casket and walked out of the room. The dead were as funny as the living, she mused as she gathered her things and got ready to head home.

She should have been home hours ago, but she'd wanted one more conversation with Nora. Perhaps Grace was going crazy. She needed to spend more time with the living, she humored herself as she headed for the parking lot and the promise of a frozen dinner from the microwave. But there had been something about Nora that made her want to go back and encourage a conversation. A bit of her wished she had known her in life. Of course, there was always a little bit of regret that went with knowing she was the last person who would ever speak to a loved one again as well.

As she opened the door to her car and tossed her bag into the passenger seat, she wondered if it were fate that had her not putting on her earphones. Would she think nothing of it had she ignored Nora Campbell? Now she wondered if she should tell Nora's family about the conversation. Perhaps she wouldn't say it was a conversation, but how would she begin letting them know the things that Nora wanted to know? It was a lot of responsibility. How many generations had received this gift? As far as she was concerned it certainly wasn't a gift—not the kind she wanted. She would think about it tomorrow.

She started the car and backed out of the parking space she thought about Matthew. She didn't watch his channel, or any channel really. She tried to stay away from anything newsworthy because it usually had a bad ending. But just to satisfy her curiosity, she would go home and Google his name. Who was Matthew Campbell, the single grandson of Nora, she mused. It was worth a minute of her time she decided as she merged onto the street and headed home.

CHAPTER 5

*E*very day of his adult life, Matthew had worn a tie. Today, however, it was choking him to death.

Since he was a young boy, he'd always expected his grandmother to pass. It was human nature. Old people died. But when the day came, he wasn't ready.

She faced death with the same dignity she faced life. She embraced every moment of it. Maybe she was just ready to go home and be with her husband. To have a love like they had, that was a goal. Matthew had no doubt his parents would see many more anniversaries. His sister had already been married for five years and had a two-year-old. There was no comparing their lives though. He had chosen his path. First, the written word had called him, and then the television cameras. There wasn't a day that went by that he didn't love his job, even in a crisis. Matthew knew that even in the bad times, he was helping people.

That might have been why he enjoyed his job as much as he did now. They let him do those fluff pieces that not everyone loved to do. He'd done the hard news. He stood outside of fires and on the street after shootings. He watched worried relatives wonder if their family member was inside a building with no way to escape. Yes, he'd much rather do those fluff pieces about a baseball bake sale than anything.

As he stood outside the mortuary waiting for his family to arrive, he wondered if Mr. Rodriguez and Mr. Leeds would be at the cemetery today. That caused him to chuckle to himself. His grandmother would expect no less of him than to find a good story to share.

He would wait until Monday to ask Grace about them again.

And what was it about Grace that had her on his mind last night? She was an attractive woman. Her job was a little odd, he thought as he brushed a piece of lint from his jacket. The one thing he had learned was that there was a job for everyone. In a few moments, he would decide if she did her job well. Though there was no doubt that she did.

He smiled as he saw his mother and father pull into the parking lot and then his mind went back to Grace. Should he tell her how grateful he was that she called to ask such a simple question of him? Certainly, the handkerchief and the bee pin were things she could have asked about when they arrived, but she hadn't. She had called him personally, and why not call his father? Maybe it was fate. He needed a distraction from Rebecca and Grace gave that to him.

His mother, dressed all in black, walked toward him with her hand stretched out. It was evident that she had been crying that morning. That too was a testament to his grandmother. How many women mourned the passing of their mothers-in-law? But Nora Campbell had been as much a mother to his mother Angela as she had been to his father.

As his mother kissed him on the cheek, he thought it would be nice to not only celebrate many anniversaries with the person that you loved but to adore their family just as much.

"Have you seen her yet?" His mother pulled back and wiped her eyes.

"No. I was waiting for everyone. Britney called and said they left home twenty minutes ago, so they should be here soon."

His father reached out his hand, and Matthew shook it before his father pulled him and hugged him. "Thanks for all your help, Matt. It's good to have someone with a good head on their shoulders to help everyone get through this."

Matthew could only give him a nod. He wasn't sure he was as brave as his father was letting on, but he wouldn't let them all know that. Again, a thirty-five-year-old man shouldn't be so distraught that his grandmother had died.

They decided to wait until the rest of the family arrived, before going inside the mortuary. Matthew thought his father was holding up just fine, but his two aunts were absolutely a wreck.

As the family filed into the lobby of the mortuary, Frank Carter greeted them. Matthew could see the resemblance between him and Grace.

He watched as Frank took the hand of one of his aunts and patted it gently. He spoke to her softly, so that not everyone heard. Whatever it was that he said, seem to bring her some peace.

"Mrs. Campbell is ready for you all. There will be an hour for visitation for all of you before guests arrive. If you are ready, I will show you to the room."

A sea of nodding heads agreed, and then they followed Frank Campbell down the hallway.

A placard on the door read Nora Campbell.

Seeing her name there tugged at Matthew's heart. He'd gone to viewings before, this was nothing new. But on the other side of the door was his grandmother. For the first time in his life, he would look at her, and she wouldn't look back with those eyes filled with love.

He cleared his throat, and his mother patted his arm. Maybe he was more of a wreck than he thought he was. At least he lived alone, and when he'd started to cry while brushing his teeth, that had been his own damn business.

Frank Carter placed his hand on the doorknob. "There is plenty of seating around the room. There are water bottles in the corner. Please feel free to write in the guestbook as well. When I open the door, she will be to the left. My family and I are here should you need anything."

With that, Frank slowly opened the door. Matthew realized they positioned his grandmother so that she wasn't the first thing they saw as they walked into the room. The sprays of flowers which had been sent caught his attention first. Then, his eyes moved to the shiny wooden box. He was far enough away that he could see there was someone in it, but for the moment he couldn't see her.

Again, he heard the cries of his aunt, and then his other aunt joined her at the casket. The rest of the family stood back as his father moved toward them.

Someone at the door caught his attention, and he turned his head to see Grace standing just outside in the hallway.

She wore a black dress and low black heels. Her dark brown hair was pulled into a low ponytail and hoops hung from her ears. Matthew wondered how many funeral dresses the woman owned.

Grace lifted her hand and gave him a small wave,

which he returned with a smile just as his mother took his arm. Together they walked toward the casket, and he could feel her shaking next to him.

"Oh, doesn't she look beautiful?"

Matthew looked down at the woman before him. He was used to seeing her smile, but there would be no more smiles. There would be no more cheek pinches or jokes at his expense, or birthday cards in the mail with a twenty-dollar bill. No, this was their new reality— a world without Grandma Nora.

Matthew wiped the tear that had formed in his eye. "She looks as though she is sleeping. I expect her to sit up at any moment and give us all hell for standing here crying over her."

His mother laughed and rested her head against his shoulder. "Mr. Carter's daughter did a beautiful job. And look," she began with a sob. "Her bumblebee pin is right where she would wear it, and her handkerchief is exactly in the right place."

Points given to Grace Carter, Matthew thought. He wouldn't tell his mother that she had called him. He let that be his secret. Then again, anyone who wasn't an absolute professional would have just added the items without as much care as Grace had.

The family spent their time with Nora, and then others began to gather. Matthew realized how honored he was to be her grandson. People hugged him and shook his hand. They all had some extraordinary story about Nora Campbell, and he felt as if he were getting to know all about his grandma.

Matthew didn't remember having all the same feelings that were flowing through him now back when his grandfather passed away. It wasn't that he loved him any less, their relationship was just different, he supposed. It had been ten years ago. His perception of the world at twenty-five was much smaller.

Grace walked through the door and silently monitored the room. He personally wanted to tell her how wonderful he thought his grandmother looked but coming in right behind her was Rebecca Barnes dressed from head to toe in black, large dark sunglasses covering her eyes, and a wide-brimmed black hat covering her blonde hair. Without even a single word, the woman had made a scene by her entrance.

Grace gave her the same warm smile Matthew had seen her give many others. A moment later, Rebecca zoned right into him and charged at him with her arms open.

She kissed him on both cheeks, and then on the mouth. There were tear streaks on her cheeks, and yet her sunglasses were so dark he couldn't see her eyes.

"I wanted to be here for you." She sobbed. "Your grandmother was such a wonderful woman. It is such a loss."

Matthew could feel the tension his mother's smile was giving off. She never much cared for Rebecca, though usually he could take or leave her. But he thought it best to usher her through, and then try and escort her out.

Rebecca took Matthew's hand and held it tightly as he walked her toward the casket. She pressed a handkerchief underneath her glasses and wiped her eyes.

"Matthew, this is so sad."

"It is. She had a very full life," he said as he looked down at his still grandmother. "She touched a lot of people. She leaves behind quite a legacy."

Rebecca sobbed again and leaned her head against his shoulder. "It's just so sad she never saw you get married or have children. You have to keep her memory alive."

Suddenly the tie around his neck grew even tighter.

Rebecca reached toward his grandmother's bumblebee pin and then retracted her hand quickly as if she realized she was about to touch a deceased person. "I never saw your grandmother without her pin."

"I don't think I did either," he admitted. "We couldn't have buried her without it."

Matthew became aware that Grace had moved in toward them as well. She greeted guests, handed out water bottles and tissues, and gave words of condolence. But did she keep looking at his grandmother as if something were off? He looked again at the pin, and it was right where he had told her to put it. The handkerchief could not have been placed any better.

His grandmother's hair looked as if she'd stepped out of the salon, and did they take the lipstick right out of her purse? What was making Grace hover around the casket?

Matthew felt the tug in his arm as Rebecca turned to sob with one of his aunts. Why wouldn't the woman just let go of him?

As he stepped to the side of the room, he watched as Grace moved to the casket. She leaned in as if she were speaking to his grandmother. Was that what people who worked with deceased did? Did they have conversations with them? Who was he to judge them? He found himself talking to his houseplant more than once.

Grace had caught his eye again and walked toward him. "Do you mind if I speak to you for a moment in the hallway?"

"Of course not," Matthew agreed as he watched her walk toward the door without him.

It seemed to be the right thing to excuse himself from Rebecca.

Grace stood in the hallway, her hands folded in front of her.

"Is there anything wrong?" he asked.

"No." Her eyes searched him for a moment and then she smiled. "I want to thank you for giving me the information last night. Again, I'm very sorry that I called you at home."

"Don't think anything of it. It was nice to hear from you."

"Oh, good. I'm glad to hear that. How does your grandmother look?"

Matthew looked into the room and immediately caught the eye of Rebecca. Would anyone have a problem if he went for a walk, he wondered.

"I think she looks beautiful. You did a fantastic job. I do, however, think I could use some fresh air. Would you care to join me?"

Whatever tension had been in Grace's shoulders seem to be relieved. "I would be happy to join you. If we go out this side door, there is a beautiful garden just around the corner."

"That sounds perfect."

CHAPTER 6

*G*race led Matthew down the hall and through the door which she had spoken about. Had he sensed her stress? She tried to make herself sparse during the viewings. Standing in the hallway usually did the trick and avoided the deceased having a conversation with her. Nora Campbell, on the other hand, was a much stronger spirit. Not only that, they had had conversations, and Grace had opened herself up to her.

One thing was absolutely sure, Nora Campbell did not care for the blonde attached to her grandson. As far as she had been concerned, her hair looked great, her dress was perfect, and the shade of paint that Grace had picked for her lips was spot on. She had guided her until the bumblebee pin was just right, and she had given her tips as to how to put a handkerchief in her sleeve. Things had been calm until the blonde showed up.

Nora had let Grace know that it bothered her that her daughters were crying. She made a comment on how handsome Matthew looked. For being a spirit that nobody else knew was around, Grace had thought that Nora was having a good time better viewing.

But when the blonde walked in and kissed her grandson, that was when Grace was pulled away from everyone else, and Nora had her attention.

"This is a beautiful garden," Matthew said, and Grace realized that she had walked all the way there without saying a word.

"It is. It was dedicated to a young man who lost his battle with cancer. His family donated." She walked down the path to the red and yellow roses, lovingly referred to as ketchup and mustard. "I've seen this garden give many families peace. That is such a wonderful gift."

"Do you have time to sit with me? On the bench?"

Because she did not have Nora in her head, she agreed.

They sat on the stone bench which had been engraved with the boy's name to whom the garden was dedicated. A gentle breeze blew through the flowers lifting their scent.

"My grandmother would've loved this. She loves roses. In fact, she has an entire garden of them."

Grace bit down on her lip. "Your sister strikes me as the kind of woman who would love roses too."

Matthew nodded before turning to look at her. "She does. You're a good judge of people."

"I see a lot of people in my work." Grace folded her hands on her lap. "Rosebushes are easily moved. Perhaps your family to consider giving your sister one of the bushes. As a memento."

A smile settled on his lips. "I think that's a beautiful idea. I'll mention it to my father. I know that would thrill my sister."

Not wanting to take credit for the idea, Grace decided she should amend her comment. "I would guess your grandmother and your sister had a conversation about it. From what I have gathered about your grandmother, she was very thoughtful like that."

"She sure was."

Grace could have stopped the conversation right there. One of Nora Campbell's wishes would have been granted, or at least brought to the surface. But now Grace was curious about the blonde that Nora didn't seem to like. How much information could she get?

"Your grandmother sure knew a lot of people. That room is full, and we have overflow in the lobby."

"She touched the lives of everyone she met. It speaks to her character."

"And the woman that is here with you was she close to grandmother?"

Matthew turned his head, his brows drawn together. "The woman that's here with me?"

"The blonde in the big hat. I saw her reach for a tissue when she came in and she seemed very distraught."

Matthew dropped his head and shook it. "I can't say she's here with me. Perhaps in support of me, but not with me."

"Oh," was all Grace could think to say.

"Rebecca is a girl that I grew up with. Somehow, she's attached herself to me, but were not an item."

Grace was happy to hear that. Perhaps when she went back inside, she could let Nora know so that she could finish delighting in her own viewing.

She was enjoying sitting outside among the roses, and she found she appreciated Matthew's conversation. Perhaps she could drag it out just a little longer.

"That piece that you did on the Boy Scouts that rescued that raccoon, it was great."

Matthew chuckled. "That was last year. It must've really struck a chord with you."

Grace grit her teeth. Honesty was always the best policy, she figured in most cases. "I looked you up on Google last night. I hope you don't mind."

"Of course not. That's how we learn about people nowadays, isn't it? Instead of asking all the normal small talk questions, we just look them up."

"That's true."

"I suppose that's why online dating works. If you put in all of your information and you can select the qualities that you like, then you don't have to have a first date. You just fly to the other one's hometown and see if you compute."

His head popped up when she giggled. "I'm sorry. That was funny."

"I think that's why I like doing the pieces that I do. I like getting to know people, ask some questions, figure out who they are."

"Me too. That's what we do here. Although the person we're trying to learn about isn't here, but you get a sense of who they were by how their family talks about them."

"Sure you get plenty of families like mine, the ones who adored the deceased, but my guess is you get the other side to that too. You know, the families that don't much care that somebody has died."

"Yes, you get that quite often. It's a little harder to deal with. Sometimes you wish you could give the deceased a voice."

"Wouldn't that be a neat trick?"

Grace gave it some thought, that was what her gift was about. Once in a while, she could let the deceased have their last word. Most of the time, however, she preferred to work without any words from the deceased. But had she not talked to Nora, would anyone have considered replanting the rose bushes at her granddaughter's house? Would they have just sold her house, roses and all? What if the new owners plowed right over them, then Nora's last wish would've been lost.

Her mouth had gone dry, and she could feel the emotion of her thoughts bubbling in her chest. She pressed her hand to her throat. "I suppose I should go back inside and make sure everything is going well."

Matthew stood. "I should too. Some of these relatives I don't remember. But Grandma would be thrilled to know that all came to see her."

Something compelled her to touch his arm. "I'm sure she knows that they're all here."

"Yeah, if there were anyone who could come and hover over their own viewing and funeral, it would be her," he said as humor lifted his voice.

It gave her some hope that perhaps if she were to share Nora's last words, he would be open to them. Of course, why him? She had all of Nora's relatives to choose from. But then again, one of Nora's last wishes was for her to invite him to dinner.

She hated to admit it, but she was intrigued enough to do so. Not today. Not tomorrow. But he had mentioned wanting to do a piece on Mr. Rodriguez and Mr. Leeds. Maybe she could make that her motivation to speak to him again.

They walked back to the door, and Matthew pulled it open for them. Grace turned to him. "I've been thinking about it. You had mentioned wanting to do a piece on the families that celebrate here."

"Right," he said as if you had jogged his memory.

"After having watched your work during my search last night, I think this would be the right piece for you. I think people would like to know that their loved ones are thought of and celebrated. Perhaps it would encourage other families to do the same."

"I think you're right. You wouldn't have time next week to talk about this, would you? Perhaps I can meet you for lunch, pick your brain a little bit."

And just like that another one of Nora Campbell's last wishes was checked off the list. "I think I would enjoy that." She pulled a business card from the pocket of her dress and handed it to him. "My cell phone numbers on the bottom. Feel free to call me."

"I will," he said as he tucked the card into his shirt pocket. "I look forward to it."

She did too, she thought as she passed by him and walked back toward the people who were there to celebrate Nora Campbell.

CHAPTER 7

*A*fter the last visitor had gone, and the family had each hugged one another and said their goodbyes, Grace walked into the room where Nora rested peacefully.

"Do I know how to throw a party or what?" Nora's voice filled Grace's ears.

"You are very loved."

"Eh, I saw a few gawkers in here. That lady that lived across the street from me, she never once spoke to me. I'm sure she just wanted to make sure I was dead so she could buy my house."

"What a horrible thought."

"I had lots of friends," Nora's voice said only to Grace. "But I had my share of enemies. You don't get this old without having pissed off a few people."

Grace laughed as she approached the casket and adjusted the bumblebee to fly just as Nora had asked her to position it. Someone must've touched it. That was no surprise.

"I spoke to Matthew about the rosebush. He knows his sister would love to have one. I think he will make sure that it happens."

"I'm sure he will. He is a doer, that grandson of mine."

"I see that in him," Grace said as she moved to pick up a few empty water bottles that had been left on the table. "You'll also be pleased to know that I'm going to have lunch with him."

Grace heard the approving hum. "So, you asked him?"

"Actually, he asked me. It's a business lunch. He wants to do a story on some of the families who visit the cemetery. He asked me to meet with him to discuss it."

"I'll take it. You're a nice girl. I'd like to see him settle down with someone like you."

"I'm flattered. You don't know anything about me though."

Again, Nora hummed in Grace's ear. "You also don't get this old without being able to read people. Take Rebecca Barnes for instance."

"And who is Rebecca Barnes?"

"That blonde I made you drive off. Oh, it burns my backside that she was here. Actually, I don't care that she was here. She's as fine as they come. I just don't like her with Matthew. She's not the right person for him."

"And you are sure they're not a couple? I watched her walk in. She kissed him right on the mouth and had her arm wrapped around him the whole time."

"No. He has in a sense in his head to know that she's not the right one. But she seems to want to dig her claws into him. I worry that the older he gets, the more he'll want to settle down. I just don't want her to wear him down. You know how women get. If they're not married by a certain age, they get very possessive."

"It's right for you to worry."

The door to the room slid open, and her brother Scott walked in. He looked around the room for a moment. "Talking to yourself again?"

"Seems like I am. Are you here to take her back?"

"Yes."

Grace turned to the casket and looked down at Nora Campbell. "I'll see you tomorrow," she whispered as she turned and left the room.

THE REST of the day was Grace's to enjoy however she wanted. It seemed as though she hadn't had an afternoon off in weeks, but she wasn't sure what she wanted to do. It had been a while since she strolled through Olde Town with its quaint shops which always brought her joy.

Perhaps that's what she would do. She would get herself fancy coffee, by that new book she'd meant to get, and window shop in all of the antique stores. The outing would be more fun if she had a friend to share it with, but her friends were still at work, so she would enjoy the time to herself.

She'd opted for an iced coffee swirled with chocolate. As she sipped it, she browsed through the independent bookstore. The book she had heard about was a romance, one of those happily ever afters. Dealing with death on a day-to-day basis, she craved those happy endings.

Grace searched the titles until she found the one she'd been looking for. At the checkout counter, she purchased her book and a bar of handmade lavender soap that she saw. She usually couldn't help herself with the impulse buys that they had at checkout counters.

With her coffee in one hand and her bag in the other, she headed toward the antique stores. She wasn't one to buy anything old, perhaps she was too afraid it would have an attachment to somebody else. The last thing she needed was a ghost living in her house with her, she mused to herself. She never had any attraction in that way, but why bring it on?

The dressers with their vanities, the old china plates, and the metal kitchen tins made her think of simpler times. She loved her technology, but there was something about the people who lived without it.

In the third store, she walked through, there were rows of old clothes, shoes, and jewelry. She couldn't imagine wearing someone else's clothing. The thought gave her chills. But she did enjoy looking at all the jewelry. Brooches fascinated her. She never wore them, as she thought they belonged on old women, but nonetheless, they were fascinating.

She stopped when she came to a case, and there was a bumblebee pin. Seeing it there brought an instant smile to her face and made her think of Nora Campbell. The saleswoman must've seen her stop because she hurried over to her.

"Is there anything I can take out of the case for you?"

Grace looked up at her and smiled. "The bumblebee caught my attention."

"Oh, the bumblebee," the saleswoman said as she stuck her key into the case and opened the glass. "You know they say that a bumblebee shouldn't be able to fly because of the mass of their body. And yet they do."

Grace had heard the story, and she knew it was a symbol of strength.

The woman took the pin out of the case and handed it to Grace. As she did with other people's personal items, she just let it sit in her hand for a moment to make sure there was no attachment. She didn't feel any other attachment but her own and the fact that she fell in love with the pin.

"Feel free to pin it on and look in the mirror," the woman said pointing behind her.

Grace had no interest in buying an antique, she reminded herself as she pinned the pin to her dress and studied it in the mirror.

She couldn't help but stare at her reflection and the pin, bright yellow on a sea of black. There was something to the story about the bumblebee. Did she feel empowered enough to wear a bumblebee on her lapel?

"I can take it to the counter for you and have it wrapped up if you'd like to look around more," the saleswoman offered.

Grace had all intention of telling her thank you, but she wasn't going to buy it. Instead, she found herself saying, "No need to wrap it up. I think I would like to wear it out."

The smile on the saleswoman's face lifted clear up into her eyes. "I think that's fabulous. I'll meet you at the front."

Grace followed her and paid for the pin. She decided right then and there that she would wear it tomorrow in honor of Nora Campbell.

MATTHEW KICKED his feet up onto his coffee table, turned on the baseball game, and took a long pull from his bottle of beer. He loosened his tie and let his head fell back against the couch. Mourning took a lot out of a person.

It had been nice to see his grandmother looking so well. In the last few months of her life, she had begun looking frail and pale. His mother had been right, Grace had made her look beautiful.

He lifted his head and took another pull from his beer just as the batter hit a home run. He thought about the lunch date he'd made for the following week. He was excited to do the story, but he wasn't stupid enough to think that's why he invited Grace to lunch. There was something about the woman that intrigued him, and it was more than just her job. She was compassionate and warm. She had an excellent eye for detail too. And, he would forever be grateful for her timeliness of pulling him out of situations where Rebecca was involved. The fact that she was a looker didn't hurt. Those eyes—they did something to him and so did her smile, and her touch. He laughed. Maybe he'd already fallen in love.

He dreaded tomorrow already. If just the viewing had worn him out emotionally, the funeral should be devastating. But he knew that the Carter family was there to ease the pain for everyone. They had done an excellent job so far. Perhaps that should be another story too, he thought as he took another drink of his beer. The family that laid other families to rest, now that was a story.

He set his beer on the table, pulled off his tie, and picked up his phone. With a few swipes, he opened up his notes and typed them in. The more he thought of it, the more he looked forward to lunch next week with Grace.

Just as he finished typing in his notes, he received a text message.

Thought you could use some company. I'm just down the street, and I have dinner. I will be there in five. XOXO Rebecca

He considered turning off the TV in closing all of the blinds, but he knew his text would be marked as read. What were the chances that Grace might need him for something? If he was swift enough perhaps he could call her or text her and tell her to meet him somewhere.

Matthew scrubbed his hand over his face. Now he was just being stupid. The Carters were well trained to take care of families. It was their job to give comfort, and they had done just that. He was finding he was getting way too attached. Wasn't he going to seem like a fool if he asked her out for more than the lunch next week?

There was no reason to reject Rebecca's invitations, warranted or not. She wasn't a threat to anything, and in his heart, he knew she was just trying to help.

When the doorbell rang, he stood, took one more pull from his beer, and then answered the door.

CHAPTER 8

*M*atthew's alarm went off on his phone at seven o'clock. On any other day, he would've been at work long before then, but on the day that he would bury his grandmother, he slept in. As he wiped the sleep from his eyes, Rebecca's arm draped over him.

Perhaps he had thought it was a dream that she had not left after dinner. He guessed he must've been pretty low, emotionally, to agree to her staying. He wasn't sure what he was worried about. Sure, they had kissed a little bit, but then they had fallen asleep. It wasn't as if they had slept together. Okay, they had slept together, but they hadn't had sex. But was that what she was going to expect? He was stupid to think that she would simply go away if he kissed her and let her sleep in his bed.

Rebecca rolled over and kissed him on the cheek. "Good morning, sweetheart."

"Morning," he said biting back any further words.

"This was nice. I can't remember when I've slept so well."

"Good. I'm going to have to get up now and get

ready. I'm supposed to be over at my parents' house by nine."

Rebecca brushed her blonde hair away from her face and smiled up at him. "I suppose I should get home and get ready for the funeral. Is there anything I can do for you or your family?"

He wanted to tell her not to show up, and that would help, but he figured he was in too deep now. He was going to have to backtrack quite a bit to get rid of Rebecca Barnes. Today wasn't the day to think about it. Today was the day to bury his grandmother and console his family. Monday morning, everything would go back to normal, minus the occasional phone call from his grandmother, or card, or home-made cookies. Thinking about it was just depressing him.

Matthew pushed back the sheets and rolled out from underneath Rebecca's arm. "I need to get in the shower. Feel free to let yourself out. The door locks automatically."

It might've been a cold way to leave a woman in his bed, but he didn't have time to think about that either.

Matthew decided he should be grateful that Rebecca tapped on the door and told him she was leaving. Luckily, she hadn't decided to peek her head in, and he no longer needed to strain his ears to listen if she left.

As he tilted his head into the warm water, he wondered what the hell he'd been thinking. Like any man who ended up in bed with a woman, sexually or not, he wasn't thinking at all.

Rebecca was a fine friend, he thought as he soaped up to his hair. But that's as far as it went. He didn't want to date her. He didn't want to sleep with her. And he most certainly did not want to marry her, which is what he feared she was looking for.

No, his mind seemed to wander elsewhere lately. It had been wandering to that cute brunette in funeral black. And that too, he decided as he rinsed his hair, was a stupid thought. Just as he had thought last night, her family was trying to take care of those who were mourning, and the Campbell family was mourning.

Regardless of that, he was still good to meet her for lunch next week. In fact, he was quite looking forward to it. Slathering the bar of soap between his hands, he gave it some thought. Maybe there was some interest there. Did someone who spent all her time with dead people have friends among the living? The very idea made him laugh. Of course, she had friends. She was too lovely not to.

Matthew focused on finishing his shower and getting a good clean shave. He dressed again in his black suit, but this time he chose a bright blue shirt to go under his jacket. The black tie he wore had been purchased by his grandmother for his birthday. The tie clip, which he slid on and adjusted, had belonged to his grandfather.

After getting himself an examination in the mirror, he thought perhaps he'd retire the suit in the back of his closet for many years. He hoped he wouldn't need it again for a very long time.

MATTHEW ARRIVED AT HIS PARENTS' house just before nine. He parked down the street since everyone had beat him there. Today, though his aunts both looked sad, there were no tears— yet.

Two limousines were waiting outside of the

house. They would take the family to the church and then to the cemetery.

The ride to the church was quiet. Matthew had to assume everybody had thoughts about his grandmother going on in their head. He was guilty of the same.

He couldn't help but wonder if she knew all the things that were going on now that she had passed. She had told him to put her in that dress, but did she think she looked okay? Would she know that the bumblebee pin was not the one his grandfather had given her? And did she like all of the arrangements that other people had sent to the mortuary?

The thought made him smile, and she looked out the window as they parked in front of the church. There would be no way to explain why the idea humored him.

The driver got out of the car and walked around the front. Then, he opened the doors for his passengers. Matthew stepped out and held his hand out for his mother.

"Thank you, son. By the way, you look very handsome," she said as she patted his cheek with her hand.

"Thank you. I decided to put the suit in the back of my closet when I get home. I don't want to wear it for quite a while."

She laughed. "I thought the same thing of this dress. I have a bag to donate to the Salvation Army. I think I might just slip it inside."

"I'll buy you a bright and beautiful dress to replace it," he offered as he gave his mother his arm and escorted her into the church.

GRACE HAD HEARD the exchange between mother and son as she gathered arrangements from the van out front. What a beautiful sentiment, she had thought. Matthew indeed seemed like quite a gentleman.

As she picked up the arrangement, she watched as Rebecca Barnes hurried down the street and toward the family. Grace let out a breath. Nora had already had a discussion with Grace about her that morning. She'd been furious because the deceased always knew things, Grace understood.

Rebecca Barnes spent the night with Matthew, and his grandmother was none too happy about it. Grace found that she was not too pleased about it either. How had she let herself even get worked up over it? Matthew Campbell was a client. Funerals were a business. And her family was very good at making people comfortable while they did business.

But she had to admit she was attracted to him, and it probably hadn't helped that Nora Campbell was insistent that she invite him out. Oh, and the comment about the veil— that weighed heavily on her mind.

However, none of it should be weighing on her mind. She should be thinking about what she was there to do.

She had made sure Nora looked as beautiful today as she had yesterday. Except for the two arrangements she was carrying in, the church was ready for the funeral. And, admittedly, even Grace was going to be devastated the moment they closed the casket for the final time. She had thoroughly enjoyed Nora Campbell's visits.

"Can I help you with those?" Matthew's voice came from behind her.

She spun and turned nearly right into him almost crushing the arrangement between them.

"I'm sorry. I guess you startled me."

"I certainly didn't mean to. Here let me take that,"

he offered as he took the arrangement from her. "Oh, I love your bumblebee pin. Did you have that on yesterday?"

Grace looked down at the pin on her dress. "I found it at an antique store yesterday. It made me think of your grandmother. I thought it was a nice way to honor her. I hope you don't mind."

"Mind? Goodness, why that I mind? I think that is a beautiful tribute."

"Thank you and thank you for your help. I had wanted to have all of this put together before you even got here."

He flashed her a smile that zapped her right in the heart. "Between you and me," he said as he leaned in closer. "I'd much rather be doing this and sitting in there. I've already seen most of the people that are going to be here today, and there's one guest, in particular, that has already arrived, and I'm not much in the mood for her."

Grace's mouth went dry. "I want to be catty, and ask who it is. But my professionalism is smacking me from the inside," she joked with a smile.

"Well, since you're on staff, maybe I should tell you who it is, and you can work to keep her away from me."

Grace swallowed hard. "Whatever I can do to make this an easier experience for you. Who do you need to make me disappear?"

A devilish clean flashed in his eyes as he leaned in closer. "Her name is Rebecca Barnes," he said as if he were passing off secret intelligence. "Tall blonde, big hat." He eased back, and the grin was bigger.

"I thought that was your girlfriend."

She was sure she didn't imagine the snarl on his lip. "I think she thinks she's my girlfriend, as I told you yesterday. But she's not," he whispered the last little bit. "Of course after last night, I'm sure she thinks we're getting married."

And with those words, Grace felt as though someone had socked her in the stomach. She had wanted Nora to have been wrong about everything, but it looked as if she were right.

Grace straightened her shoulders. "Honestly, do you need me to make her leave?"

He actually gave it some thought she humored before he leaned in closer again. "I'll tell you what. If you see her next to me or touching me, maybe you could need my assistance. I'm sure I could break away to answer any question you might have." He winked.

"Okay. If it's an opportunity in which I can help, I'll come to your rescue."

"That's my girl," he said giving her a wink and a playful punch to the jaw, as one might have in an old movie to say *that's swell kid*. Then he turned to walk into the church with the arrangement he'd taken.

Grace took another moment before she followed him. She didn't like that him winking at her made her heart flutter. Perhaps it was a good thing Nora wouldn't be speaking to her anymore. She wasn't sure what she was going to do with the interests that had sparked in this man.

CHAPTER 9

*T*he arrangements were set at the front of the church near and around Nora's casket which remained open for viewing.

Grace could hear Nora's humming in aggravation. She wanted to assure her that her worries were invalid. However, Nora's family was surrounding her.

"That Rebecca is here, and she's holding hands with Matthew."

Grace turned to one of the arrangements and made it look as though she were fixing it. "I have inside information, he's not with her," she whispered.

"A woman spending the night with a man usually means they're involved."

With a glance to her side, Grace continued fixing the arrangement. "It's a different game nowadays. Regardless, his heart isn't in it. He's asked me to keep her from him."

As she turned to look at a different arrangement, once again she found herself running right into Matthew.

He was smiling, widely. "Do you talk to the flower arrangements? Does it make them behave?"

Grace forced a smile on her lips. "Sometimes

when you work with people who don't talk back, you find that talking to inanimate objects is normal."

Matthew laughed and touched her arm. "I like your sense of humor. I'm sure it's a good thing to have in your line of work."

"Oh, it is."

As Matthew walked toward his family and sat in the first pew, Grace moved on to another arrangement.

"Oh, honey, I think I was wrong to be upset."

Grace looked over at Nora resting peacefully in the casket. "And why do you say that?" she whispered toward the flowers.

"Because I saw how my grandson just looked at you. He even touched your arm. Oh, happy day. I think I made my match. I'm ready to go on."

Grace's father approached her. "I think everybody's ready. They're going to open the doors. I'll escort the family out. Your brother has all of the pamphlets for you to hand out."

Grace nodded. "Okay. I'm almost done with this arrangement."

She listened as her father instructed the family to what they were doing next. Finishing with the arrangement, she stopped one last time by the casket. "By the way, Nora, it's been wonderful to talk to you."

Precisely on schedule, her father opened the doors to guests, and the church filled. Grace could hear all the stories being told around her as people reminisced about Nora Campbell.

Some of the guests made their way to the casket, and they too spoke to her. Grace wondered if any of them heard the things that Nora had to say back.

When it was time, her father gathered the family, and they followed the minister into the church.

Grace watched as Mathew held his mother's hand.

As the family sat down in the pews, Grace noticed that Rebecca Barnes sat directly behind Matthew. She winced as Rebecca placed her hand on his shoulder. She supposed there were a time and place where she could interrupt, and this wasn't one of them. Nora was going to have to deal with the fact that Rebecca was going to be there. Even in death, you were guaranteed everything.

Grace, her brother, and her father stood at the back of the church during the funeral. Their mother was at the cemetery overseeing final preparations.

She had caught Matthew turning twice to smile at her. It seemed a little strange to be flirting with somebody at their grandmother's funeral, but she was enjoying herself. And, she had to admit to herself, it was fun to watch Rebecca Barnes turn to see what he was looking at.

When the funeral was over, Grace's father and brother started toward the casket to close it and remove it. Before they closed the lid, Grace heard Nora's voice one last time. "Thank you, darling. Thank you for passing on my last goodbyes. It was nice to meet you. Take care of my family."

Usually at funerals, Grace didn't cry. She'd attended more funerals than she had weddings or graduations. Death was the assured part of life, and though it was a sad time for many, she had seen it too often to cry. But not today. Tears welled in her eyes, and she quickly pushed him away. If it had only been a stray tear, that would've made sense, but this was going to be a flood.

Squeezing her eyes closed, she hoped no one saw her. But when she opened them again, and the flood poured down her cheeks, she saw the concerned look that Matthew gave her. Without thinking about what she was supposed to do next, she turned and ran out of the church and to the car.

Her father and brother slid the casket into the back of the hearse. It was one of those things that they liked to have done before the family came out of the church. There were a few things that made funerals easier, and that seemed to be one of them.

Frank had looked at her as if to say, *what are you doing?* But he said nothing. Instead, he gave her a nod and walked back into the church.

MATTHEW WATCHED as Grace hurried from the church, with Rebecca's hand still on his shoulder. He wondered what had happened. Surely she wasn't sad about his grandmother. She had to be immune to that, right? But what if she wasn't? What if every funeral that she attended affected her in that way?

He was undoubtedly going to need to do a story on her now, he decided. He thought the compassion was all an act, the gracious in its execution. But watching her rub away tears and then leaving the church as she did, that was more than compassion. He didn't know what else to call it, but it was more. He retook his mother's hand and escorted her from the church. Part of him wanted to get outside and find Grace.

Matthew noticed that Grace's brother had come into the church and began to take out the arrangements. He knew they would also be at the cemetery, but he thought perhaps she would carry them out.

When he got outside, people came toward him. Again, he was hugged and kissed by strangers who loved his grandmother. He never did see Grace.

Time spun away, and he and his family were back

in the limo following the hearse to the cemetery. This time the drive wasn't as quiet. Now his father spoke of appointments he had to make the next week to begin closing out his grandmother's estate. His mother made a comment to the fact that she and his aunts were going to go through her kitchen that weekend and take the food items. Silently he agreed, there was no need to let them all go to waste.

"Matthew, are you okay, sweetheart?"

He turned to look at his mother next to him.

"I asked if you would like to come and help us tomorrow."

"Oh," he began, realizing he had been paying any attention. "Yeah, I'd be happy to do that. Do you mind if I take up one of the rosebushes? I know that Brittany would like one. I think Grandma promised her one. I'll ask her about it, but I think that was the deal." He realized he was rambling.

His mother's face softened with a smile. "I think that is lovely. I suppose there's a rosebush for everyone. Your grandmother did love her roses."

Matthew gave her an absent nod and looked out the window.

"Did you see that the daughter had a bumblebee pin on?" His father asked.

His mother turned toward his father. "I did. I was afraid she had stolen your mother's, but your mother had hers on too."

Matthew looked at his parents. "She saw it in an antique store yesterday and thought of Grandma. She wore in tribute. I told her I thought it was very nice. I hope no one else minded."

His mother placed her hands on her heart and sighed. "That family has been so wonderful to us. What a beautiful tribute. I'll make sure to tell her I thought it was nice."

Matthew nodded and looked back out the window. He sincerely hoped Grace would be at the cemetery when they got there. He wasn't quite sure why it bothered him as much as it did that she'd hurried out of the church, but it did. He took in a deep breath and let it out slowly. He was overthinking it, but Grace Carter was weighing heavy on his mind.

CHAPTER 10

$\mathcal{T}$he procession into the cemetery was slow. The two limousines followed the hearse around the corners.

Matthew immediately saw the two men who would gather for baseball games. They stood as his grandmother passed, each of them taking off the baseball caps and placing them over their hearts. The darkness of the windows of the limousine would never have allowed the men to see him wave, but he did. Matthew appreciated the sentiment. He looked forward to meeting them.

Up ahead he could see the tent that covered his grandmother's final resting place. Chairs were set in rows next to the grave so that they could have one more ceremony.

At that moment, Matthew decided he didn't want any of this pomp and circumstance when he passed away. There had to be a more natural way to he buried.

The van which had been parked outside of the church pulled up, and he knew that the flower arrangements were inside. He hoped that Grace was too. As the driver opened the doors to the limousine,

Matthew stepped out and again helped his mother out. He watched as Grace's father stepped out of the hearse, and her brother out of the van with the arrangements.

The passenger door opened; however, it wasn't Grace that stepped out. It was her mother.

Matthew escorted his mother and his aunt to their seats next to the grave, and he returned toward the hearse with the other pallbearers. From there he watched Grace's brother, and mother carry the arrangements toward the grave site.

The process was the same as any other funeral he'd ever been to. The family and guests gathered around the grave, and Matthew and the other pallbearers carried his grandmother to her final resting spot. The minister spoke for a few minutes more and then placed a rose atop her casket.

Rebecca had managed to weave her way through the guests, and stood behind him, both of her hands on his shoulders. For the moment the contact gave him comfort. He wasn't sure why. Perhaps it was because she was a friend, even if he had absolutely no interest in her whatsoever. But his mind kept going back to watching Grace hurry out of the church.

He wondered if anyone had said to her about the bumblebee pin. Maybe someone else didn't think it was as compassionate as he did. Could they have said something that hurt her feelings?

She certainly didn't seem like the kind of girl who would be hurt and runoff by somebody saying something, but then again, he didn't know her at all. And as Rebecca gave his shoulder a squeeze, he realized he did want to know her better.

GRACE HAD SEEN the funeral procession as it passed

by the mortuary door. Her brother had dropped her off and picked up their mother. She had become much too emotional, and there was no way she could handle herself at the cemetery.

She wasn't quite sure of herself sitting in the office either. Not once in her entire life, even when her own grandparents had passed away, had she acted like she did today.

But the sincerity of Nora Campbell's words had taken her over that edge. They had made her realize that the gifts she had could be more than a burden. They were a gift and an awesome responsibility.

She thought about the book she had tucked away in her desk with the combination to Mr. Jackson safe, and Mrs. Rodriguez's list. For them, those had been their last goodbyes, and Grace had not done anything with them. What if that was her calling? What if she were supposed to give people closure on both sides?

She reached for a tissue and dabbed her eyes. It was too much to think about.

For a moment she thought about the look Matthew gave her when he turned around that last time at the funeral. She couldn't help but wonder what he thought. Would he call next week for lunch? Would he still be interested in the stories of the people around the cemetery? Nora had led her to believe that if he were to learn of Grace's messages to others, he would understand. Was that true? Or would she think she was some kind of freak?

Grace glanced at the clock on the wall. Tonya was due at any moment, and Grace would have the weekend off. For the first time in her life, she wanted to do was lock herself in her house, bury herself under mounds of blankets, and watch old movies. For some reason the moment that Nora said goodbye, her heart had broken.

. . .

MATTHEW STOOD at the side of his grandmother's casket, with Rebecca's hand in his. He placed his hand atop the lid and closed his eyes. If he whispered to her would she hear? Did she know the things he was thinking? If anyone in the world, or in heaven, could be spiritually present, he knew it was his grandmother.

As the guests and family made their way back to their cars, Matthew wondered if she should ask about Grace. He decided it wouldn't hurt, so he excused himself from Rebecca and walked toward Grace's mother.

"Mrs. Carter," he called to her, and she turned to him.

"Mr. Campbell, I hope that everything went as planned today. Your grandmother looked very peaceful."

"She did. Your daughter did a remarkable job. Even my mother said so."

Grace's mother reached out and touched his arm. "I will let her know. She takes great pride in her work."

"I was hoping she would be here," he said. "I saw her at the church and spoke to her briefly."

He noticed a line formed between Mrs. Carter's brows. "I'm not sure she was feeling well. Her brother dropped her off and picked me up on the way to the cemetery."

Matthew nodded. Perhaps that was all it was. "I hope she feels better. Again, on behalf of my family, we'd like to thank you for everything your family has done for us. It won't be easy to be without my grandmother, but we feel as though through the graciousness of your family this transition will not be as hard."

Mrs. Carter pressed her hand to her chest, just has his own mother had done earlier. "That is exactly what we want to hear. Thank you for that."

Matthew gave her a smile and turned back toward the limousine that would carry his family home. Rebecca waited just beyond the guests who had gathered. She waved, and he gave her a nod. Tonight, he thought perhaps he would stay at his parents' house. He certainly didn't want any extra house guests, because he wasn't sure what kind of mindset he was in.

CHAPTER 11

*T*he coffee could've been stronger. Grace thought as she took another sip. Just as she swallowed, she yawned. Seriously, how was sitting on the couch all weekend doing nothing making her so tired on Monday morning?

She sipped the coffee again and looked down at the files in front of her. Juan was finishing up with a Bertha Gordon, age ninety-two. The file had a picture of Bertha on her last birthday, and she appeared to be happy and healthy. The notes said that she had passed in her own bed during the night. No sickness. No injuries.

Grace hoped that when her last day came, she too would just slip off to sleep. It was as if nature said *your time is up.*

As she picked up the photo, she studied it, as she did with each of the people she worked on. However, this time she wondered if Bertha had more to her story.

Grace bit the inside of her cheek as she thought about Nora Campbell's last goodbyes. Would Bertha have a list of goodbyes too?

She'd never made it her business or her priority to

speak to those she worked on. She'd made it a deliberate practice to never be able to hear them at all. But all of that had changed when she'd been distracted and walked into the room with Nora Campbell.

Juan walked past the room where Grace sat alone looking at the file. "Mrs. Gordon is all ready for you, sweetheart."

Grace looked up at the man who smiled back at her. "Thank you."

He didn't walk on but remained in the doorway looking at her. "You doin' okay? Got a long look about you."

"Just doing some contemplation."

She thought that would have given him enough information and he would have walked on as he usually did. Juan wasn't much for conversation, and she assumed that was why he'd chosen his profession.

"This kind of work makes you contemplate a lot of things. We see the good. We see the bad," he offered as he pulled out a chair and sat down. "I have a journal in my car, one in my nightstand, and one in my desk. Somedays I just need to empty myself onto the pages to get past daily death."

Grace eased back in her chair. The man was full of wisdom, and she hadn't expected it. "I think that's a great idea. I might have to try that."

He gave her a wink, as he often did. "Mrs. Gordon troubling you?" He looked at the file.

"I was just considering her age and that she passed in her sleep. I think I'd like that best when my time is up."

Juan nodded slowly as if he were thinking about what she said. "I always thought dying midst doing something you loved would be awesome." He chuckled. "I don't mean falling off the mountain you're climbing, but maybe once you'd descended from the peak, and you're looking up at what you'd accomplished."

He had a point, she thought. But she still thought dying in bed during her sleep was the way to go.

Juan gave her arm a pat. "I've been doing this a long time, and so have your folks. We're all here if you need to talk and we have a long list of people for you to talk to if you need it too. You can't do this job day in and day out without facing your own mortality. I get it."

"Thanks," Grace said as Juan stood to leave. "I appreciate it."

This time he gave her that smile that always set her at ease as he stood and walked out of the room.

Grace sat there for a few more moments looking down at the folder. Reaching into the pocket of her apron, she pulled out her headphones. Studying them, she considered what she had to offer to Mrs. Gordon. All of the others had caught her off guard. They had spoken to her when she had forgotten the simple step of blocking them out. She owed nothing to anyone. Those who had entrusted her with goodbyes, or secrets, had done so on their own accord. But what she was considering was to walk into Mrs. Gordon, unprotected. If Mrs. Gordon chose to speak to her, it would be Grace's fault, and anything she was entrusted with would be her responsibility.

For just a moment she thought of Nora Campbell. One of the rosebushes outside her house would be transplanted at her granddaughter's home, all because Grace had reminded them about it. There was still the matter of the key to the lockbox and the veil. She'd see how things went if she spoke to Matthew. Otherwise, she would attend to those other last wishes as well. After all, she had gone back in to talk to Nora Campbell, and it wasn't an accident.

Tucking her headphones back into her pocket, Grace stood from the table and picked up the files. As she walked down the hall toward the room where Mrs. Gordon waited, Tonya flagged her down to the front desk.

"These just arrived for you," she said as she handed her a bouquet of mixed flowers.

"For me? Are you sure?"

"They say for Grace Carter. We don't have any current *guests* with your name."

Grace set the arrangement on the counter and removed the card from its plastic fork in the center.

Thank you for all you did for my family. I look forward to seeing you soon. Matthew

Grace swallowed hard. "Did my parents get a bouquet too?"

Tonya smiled as she sat back in her chair. "Nope. Just you. You must've made a good impression."

She would have thought exactly the opposite. She didn't even go to the graveside service. Without another word, she picked up the bouquet and started back down the hall to the room where Mrs. Gordon waited.

She supposed she could have taken the flowers and put them in the break room. They would have died in her car. Instead, she decided to keep them in the room with her. Maybe Mrs. Gordon would enjoy them too.

The bouquet in her hand and the file tucked under her arm, Grace opened the door. Bertha Gordon was laid out on the table just as Grace had expected. Her skin was that gray color that came with death and her hair undone after having been washed.

By the time Grace was done, she would look as if she were sleeping.

"Those are beautiful flowers. I absolutely love sunflowers, don't you?" A woman's voice filter graces ears.

"I do love them. I just received them. It was a nice surprise," she said as she walked toward Bertha Gordon. "I've come to do your hair and makeup. Is there anything you would like me to know that would make your family more comfortable with your appearance?"

"I have a wig. See that mop on top of my head? I don't like it. I like my wig."

Grace took a pen from the pocket of her apron and made a note on the file she carried in. "I will ask about it. Sometimes family stops thinking about those little pieces. Especially if it was something you did on your own, without any help."

"Oh, I did everything on my own, sweetheart. That body you see there, it looks old, but my mind was young."

Her words resonated with Grace. That was precisely what she wanted. She knew bodies aged, and she'd seen enough of them to realize they all aged differently. What Grace wanted more than anything was to stay sharp until her very last day.

Since Grace had decided to go into the room fully expecting to have a conversation with Bertha, she decided to get to know the woman. "I'm going to start with your makeup," Grace informed her as she set the file on the counter. "Do you have a certain lip color you like best?"

She heard Bertha laugh. "I love peach. Oh, it is a dreadful color on my skin tone, but I love it, love it, love it."

Grace picked up the colors that she would put on first as a foundation. "Then peach it shall be."

"I expect that my daughter-in-law will want to wipe it off. Don't you let her."

"We will make sure that the last color on your lips, regardless of what happens between now and then, is peach."

"I do like your style," Bertha said as Grace began to apply foundation to her pale gray skin. "I wore makeup every day until I died. Don't think I was out to impress anyone. I did it because it made me feel good. I wore all my jewelry at one time, and usually had my fingernails painted bright red."

Grace noticed that Bertha's fingernails were natural. "Do you have a special red that you like the most?"

"Not really. I just like me some red fingernails."

Grace chuckled at the woman's funny accent. Even in death people had a sense of humor. "I have a favorite red. I will bring it and make sure your fingernails look perfect."

Grace stepped back to look at the foundation she had put on Bertha just as her phone rang in her pocket.

"His grandmother says to tell him not to mess this up," Bertha said as Grace looked at the ID on her phone.

Because she had called Matthew the other night, his name came up on the display. She shifted a glance back to the table as if Bertha were going to be sitting there smiling up at her. Of course, she didn't, but Grace could hear laughter in her ears.

Deciding that if Nora could talk through Bertha, she would take the call in the hallway.

MATTHEW LISTENED to the ringing on the other end

of the phone and wondered if she'd answer—and then she did.

"Hi," he said when he realized she'd called him by name when she'd answered. "How did you know it was me?"

"I had your number in my phone from the other night."

He'd forgotten she'd called him. He owed her big for that too. Since then, he'd been avoiding Rebecca like the plague.

"Right. I wanted to call and see about setting up a time to talk to you about that story we talked about. And, I'd like to talk to you about doing a story on your family as well."

"My family?"

"Yes. I think the compassion you give to grieving families is outstanding. I'd like to share that with the community."

"Wow. I didn't expect that." Her voice carried sweetly through the phone to his ear. "That would be very special."

"Do you have time for lunch tomorrow?" It might be too soon, but he couldn't help but think of her and hoped she'd want to see him.

"Tomorrow?" she repeated and hummed as if she were giving thought to it. "I have a viewing to tend to from eleven to one."

"Oh," he heard the own disappointment in his voice. "Dinner?"

She was silent for a moment before she answered. "I could do dinner. After six if that's not too late."

"That would be perfect. Can I pick you up at work or at your house?"

"That seems a little formal for business. Why don't I meet you at Bakas' on First," she suggested.

"Bakas? Can't place it."

"It's Greek."

Now he remembered. "White pillars at the front door."

"That's it. I'll meet you there at six fifteen?"

"I look forward to it," he said easing back in his chair thinking about seeing her again.

"Oh, and Matthew, thank you for the flowers. That was very thoughtful of you and your family."

He winced at the family part. Specifically, he hadn't put them on the card so that she would know they were just from him, but he understood why she'd have thought that.

"My pleasure," he said. "We appreciate all you did for us last week."

They said their goodbyes, and Matthew set his phone on the table next to him and laced his fingers behind his head.

He'd never looked so forward to seeing someone, as he was Grace. He had to admit there were a lot of false pretenses to his meeting. The story on the people at the cemetery and one on her family were factual and going to be hits. He knew it. But they were just the gateway to getting to know her.

His grandmother would have loved her, he was sure. She'd come to him in a dream the night before and urged him to call Grace. He'd planned on doing so, but the urging from the dream kept it in the front of his mind.

A dream was just a dream—a subconscious thought, but it had meant a lot to him. Every day that passed he missed his grandmother a little more. Seeing her in his dreams was a blessing.

CHAPTER 12

*M*rs. Gordon's granddaughter had arrived with the wig her grandmother wore most often. "I can't believe we didn't even think about bringing it when we brought her clothes. She never went out in public without it."

Grace smiled sweetly as she took the wig. She'd known for a fact that Bertha Gordon didn't leave the house without her hair. Bertha had given her quite the dissertation while Grace had painted her fingernails with OPI Red.

"I'll make sure she looks as if she's going out when you see her."

"That'll make her happy. She wasn't vain, she just like looking her best."

And that Grace knew too.

The moment Grace walked back into the room with Bertha Gordon she heard the cheering in her ears. "They brought it. Oh, that makes me so happy. I'm going to assume my granddaughter brought my wig, she's the one that would think of these things."

"She certainly did. Nice lady."

"Yeah, she's not like her mother, the one that will wipe off the peach lipstick."

"I promised you, you'll have peach forever," Grace said as she moved to Bertha and skillfully put on her wig and adjusted it. "I'll get it just right and make final adjustments as well."

"I already look better," Bertha said in her ear.

"Bertha," Grace said aloud to the room which was sans other living people. "Was Nora Campbell with you earlier when she gave me the message about Matthew?"

"I could hear her."

Grace contemplated that. Perhaps Nora Campbell would never speak directly to Grace again, now that her body, the single vessel that carried her soul was gone, but would she always talk through someone else?

"You look beautiful," Grace said to Bertha as she took a step back and looked down at the woman. "Any last wishes?" she asked, though she wasn't sure she knew why she'd done so. She didn't want to make it a habit of having extra things to do for people.

"Sweetheart, you've done a great job with me. I lived a long and full life. I think I took care of all my business. My only wish is for everyone to live a long and happy life like I did. Find love, honey. Embrace it and pass it on."

Grace could feel the tears sting her eyes as she batted them away. "I will do that."

"Yes, you most certainly will. Goodbye," Bertha Gordon said and Grace realized she could feel her leave.

She stood there for a few more moments looking down at the small woman who had lived a long and happy life, as she'd said. Grace was delighted she'd made the decision to communicate with her and learn about her. At that moment, she felt peace in her heart and had a greater appreciation for what she did every day.

SATURDAY MORNING GRACE set to work on a young mother who had lost her battle with cancer. She'd gone in without her earphones, again on purpose, and then wished that she hadn't.

The woman cried, and in death was mourning her own children whom she'd left behind at three and seven.

Grace felt the ache in her own chest and had shed a few tears of her own. The woman didn't ask for anything special, only to be made beautiful for her daughters to see her one last time. That was something that Grace could promise.

When the door to the room opened, Grace's mother walked in and leaned up against it. "That woman is going to get on my last nerve."

"Who's that?" Grace asked as she added eyebrows to the young mother.

"Mrs. Gordon's daughter-in-law."

Grace let out a little laugh. "Let me guess. She doesn't like the lipstick?"

"How did you know that?" Grace let her mother's question linger there a moment before her mother let out a breath. "Oh, you spoke to Bertha Gordon?"

"I did. She wants the peach lipstick, and I told her that for eternity she would wear it, and not to worry."

A smile formed on her mother's lips. "I think that is an extraordinary thing you promised her."

"Least I could do. If they want it removed, for now, we can do that. But in the end, Bertha gets what she wants."

Her mother moved to her and rested her hand on

BERNADETTE MARIE

her shoulder. "This one is unfortunate," she said looking down at the young mother.

"She's very sad. She wants to look extra special for her daughters."

Grace heard her mother sniff. "She looks like a sleeping princess." And that was met with approval from the sobbing mother who lay still in front of them. "Maybe you should remember to put in your earphones. Or the offer to work the front desk is still open."

As Grace examined the work she'd already done, she shook her head. "Not now. I think this is where I'm supposed to be for now."

"I don't want anyone getting into your head. Not everyone has a good disposition in death."

Grace agreed with a nod. "I'll be careful." She picked up her lip color pallet and heard the voice of the sobbing mother tell her that she liked the pearl pink color. With a nod, she began to drag her brush through the color and apply it to her lips. "By the way, I'm going to meet Matthew Campbell for dinner tonight. He wants to do a story on the families at the cemetery. Specifically, I think he wants to know about Mr. Leeds and Mr. Rodriguez before he approaches them."

"Good time to catch them too. Double-header this weekend. They'll be there all day."

"Good to know. He also mentioned doing a story on us, the family. He thinks what we do is very honorable and helpful to those who have lost a loved one."

Her mother clasped her hands together. "I love it. Do you want someone to go with you? You don't know Matthew Campbell. I don't know if you should be meeting a man you don't know."

80

Shaking her head, Grace turned to her mother. "I'm thirty-years-old. I'm meeting him there. I'm not getting into his car. I'm not showing him where I live. And it's a public place. I'll be fine."

"You call when you get home."

"I will."

Her mother let out a long breath. "Okay. Well, I suppose I'll go back out there. I'm going to guess the rest of the family doesn't much like the daughter-in-law either. I've been around grieving families a lot since I married your father. I've seen all kinds. This is the classic, *if we just ignore her* kind of situation."

"And you always handle them so well."

Her mother pumped up her shoulders and gave her salt and pepper hair a flip. "I do."

And with that, Grace was alone with the grieving mother again. "I wanted that kind of relationship with my girls. Now they won't have that."

Grace considered her words carefully as the young mother sobbed. "Is there anything I can tell them that would give you peace?"

The sobbing stopped for a moment. "I would like you to tell my oldest, her name is Kimberly, that a princess can be found in each and every girl. A princess is someone who walks with their heads high, shoulders back, and has confidence, not just someone who marries a prince."

"Okay."

"And my youngest, her name is Mabel. I want her to sing *You are My Sunshine* every night before she goes to bed because it was our song. Tell her that when she sings it, I will hear it."

A tear rolled over Grace's cheek, and she let it drop. "I would sing that with my grandmother. I will share that with them."

The woman took a few deep breaths, and Grace heard the sobbing subside. "I think I'm ready to go now. I hear my own grandmother calling for me," she said. "Thank you. I appreciate you helping my family."

And again, the room went still.

CHAPTER 13

*C*hecking his watch, again, Matthew had resigned to the fact that Grace wasn't going to show. He sipped from his second beer and decided that when he was done, he'd pay the tab and head out. It wouldn't be the first time a woman he didn't even know broke his heart.

He mused at his imaginary pain, and then it lifted when he saw her walking in. Was it his imagination, or did she look sad?

Matthew stood from his seat as she walked toward him, tucking her keys into her purse.

"I'm so sorry I'm late. I'm surprised you waited for me," she said looking up at him with those eyes, which had defiantly been crying.

"No worries. I had a few beers and did some people watching. Something every reporter loves to do. Have a seat," he offered and watched as she fidgeted with her purse again before she sat. "What can I get you to drink? Wine? Beer?"

She stared at him blankly for a moment, and then her eyes softened, and a gentle smile formed on her lips. "I'd like a white wine. Any kind is fine."

"I'll find the waitress and get you one."

Matthew stood at the bar as the waitress poured the wine and he watched Grace settle in at the table. From the large purse she'd been messing with, she pulled out a compact and powdered her face and then added lipstick.

He knew in his job that days could be trying. There were times that he'd covered a burning building and not everyone came out. Accidents on the highway were troubling because when it was over, he'd climb back into his car and drive away as they took someone out of a vehicle for the very last time. He couldn't imagine what her day to day was like when all of her clients were already deceased. What did that do to someone to be surrounded by death all the time?

Well, wasn't that the story he wanted to tell?

She was well composed when he returned with her glass of wine.

"Thank you," she said taking the glass and then a sip as he sat across from her. "This is good. I wish I knew more about wine. But I don't know anything more than red and white."

Matthew lifted his beer bottle toward her in a toast. "I only know beer. Pale, stout, and IPA."

She laughed at that and eased back in her seat. Matthew took that as a victory.

Did he dare ask her how her day was? For a man who made his living on small talk to get information, he was suddenly at a loss.

Grace sipped her wine. "I watched one of your segments this morning," she said, and he narrowed his gaze on her.

"I wasn't on this morning."

She waved off that thought with her hand. "No, I Googled you, again. Let's see, it was a piece on the birds that migrate to the lake at the museum, and all of the people who gather to watch."

Now he smiled wide. "That is a good piece. Nominated for an Emmy."

"Rightfully so," she agreed. "I only had time for one, but I know I've seen others."

"So, I suppose that stands as my resume? You've seen the kind of work I do. What do you think about me doing the piece on the families at the cemetery?"

"I think it would be a wonderful tribute." She sipped again. "I told my mom about it. She agrees. And, a little tip, there's a game tomorrow so Mr. Rodriguez and Mr. Leeds will be at the cemetery all day."

"Reporters love good tips."

She laughed easily now. Perhaps he'd been able, in his feeble way, to offer her a release for whatever stress she'd been having.

"Would you mind if I went with you to talk to them? I have tomorrow off, and the mortuary and cemetery are places I stay away from on my days off, but I'd love to have time to sit with them and hear their stories again."

"So you've sat with them before and talked?" he asked, hoping it didn't sound as if he were interviewing her.

"In passing. I've never stood and talked more than ten or fifteen minutes. I suppose, because of my position, I ease back and let the families have their personal time at the cemetery."

He nodded and finished off his beer. He'd like another, but two was always his limit.

"I admire what you do," he offered as he leaned his arms on the table. "It's a very personal thing to carry with you every day."

Running her finger over the rim of her glass, Grace shifted her eyes to meet his. "It is. It's hard." The word hard was emphasized with a drop of her shoulders, and he wondered if she even knew she'd done it. "Today I had to give a message to two little girls. One that their mother passed on to them. It took everything I had to not melt into a sobbing mess on the floor when they hugged me, and then their father hugged me too."

"That goes above and beyond your scope of work, doesn't it?"

Her eyes went wide as if perhaps he'd offended her. "My scope of work is to ease the pain of the sur-viving parties. The deceased have made their peace, usually," she said with a shrug and a bit of a wince. "What we do is to offer respect for the deceased and help the families recover from the loss. In my case, that's to make the deceased presentable so that the last memory the family has is pleasant."

Matthew sat back. "You're very good at what you do. I have to admit my grandmother looked as though she were resting peacefully—minus the snoring."

That caused her to laugh, and he was grateful she had. Perhaps he'd managed not to completely piss her off yet. He motioned to the waitress to bring them menus and water. After a few moments of scanning over the choices, they each opted for a gyro platter.

"I noticed you don't have on your bumble bee pin," he said as he caught himself gazing at her.

"I misplaced it. I didn't have it on when I took off that dress, but..." There was disappointment that shadowed her eyes.

"I'm sure it'll turn up."

Grace nodded. "I'm sure. You know how it is when you get to moving too fast in the mornings. So how are you and your family doing? I feel as if we've only talked about me."

He'd wanted it to be all about her. There was something deep inside of him that said she had quite the story. However, he'd feed the need for conversation too.

"We're all doing okay. It helps that we had a lot of years with my grandmother. We got the rosebush planted at my sister's house. I have one sitting on my porch, which I'll get planted at some point."

He saw her wince, but she didn't say anything.

"We've been going through her house. There isn't much left. She'd weeded things out over the years. There is a lockbox that we found in her closet, but we've yet to find the key," he said, and he saw the expression on her face drop, and her eyes grew wide.

"Lockbox?"

"Yeah, you know with papers in it?"

She nodded and sipped her wine. "I think you should look under the mattress for the key. Between the mattress and the box-spring." She sipped again. "I've known of a lot of people who put keys there."

He watched as she worked on composing herself. "I'll make sure to look there."

Now she smiled, but it was forced. He could read people well enough to wonder what it was she was hiding.

"Anyway, we should have things cleaned out soon. The weird thing is, my mother gave me a box with my name on it. Inside was my grandmother's wedding veil, and the bumblebee pin my grandfather had made for her."

Grace, who was mid-sip, choked on her wine. She grabbed for a napkin and coughed until tears ran down her cheeks.

"Are you okay?" Matthew moved from his seat at

the booth to the other side next to her. He wasn't sure what he could do but to pat her on the back.

She held up her hand. "I'm fine. I'm fine." She reached for the glass of water the waitress had brought for him. She drank it down and then wiped her eyes. "I'm all good."

"You're sure?"

"I'm sure."

"Anyway, I don't know what the sentiment was. But I asked my mom to take them and disburse them appropriately."

"And what did she do with them?"

"She said she'd see that they got to the right person."

CHAPTER 14

*T*he waitress brought their food to the table and sat each place in front of them, and he was still seated beside her.

"This looks delicious," Matthew said adjusting the plate in front of him and not moving back to the other side of the table.

Grace took in a few more deep breaths and sipped the water again. Had this business meeting just turned into a full on date? Well, of course, it had turned into a date, and somehow from the other side, his grandmother had arranged it.

There was no way Nora Campbell knew about her before she passed. Why had she given Matthew the veil and the bumblebee pin? Was she a hopeful spirit making Grace crazy from the beyond? Was she also clairvoyant and knew who she'd be in touch with?

"Aren't you going to eat?" Matthew asked, his mouth full of his first bite of the gyro.

"Yes," she said placing her napkin in her lap. "My mind was wandering."

"I would think in your line of work that would

happen. I mean you're with someone, but they're really not talking back to you, right?"

She turned to him as her heartbeat thudded in her chest. "Why do you say that?"

He stopped mid-bite looking at her as horrified as she must have looked at him. "It was a joke. Your *people* don't talk to you. It must be lonely," he restated his meaning and observed her.

Readjusting the smile on her face, she nodded. "Right. It's lonely." God, could she seem more spastic in front of the man?

She needed to lighten up. It wasn't as if she were going to sit there and tell the man she could talk to the dead. And, in fact, she'd had great conversations with his grandmother. She knew about the key to the lockbox, the rose bush, the veil, and the pin. If she sat there and told him that, she'd be locked up the next day.

The problem was, she really liked him. She wanted this dinner to be more than just a business dinner to discuss his fluff piece on the news. Sure, she was a little standoffish, but she couldn't help it. Or could she?

Grace took a bite of her dinner. "This is my favorite place for gyros. This and a little stand on the pedestrian mall."

"I've had those. Not bad," he offered as he dipped one of his french fries in the ketchup. "What time do the men get to the cemetery before the games?"

Okay, this was more comfortable. She could talk about work. "Not too much earlier. They show up at the start and leave at the end. Rain or shine."

He nodded as if he were taking mental notes. "I think I'll come a little early and take some flowers to my grandmother."

"She'd appreciate that," she said and then held her breath.

"I think she would."

Grace let out the breath and took another bit.

Matthew set down his gyro and sipped from his glass of water before putting it back on the table between them. "I don't want you to think I'm crazy, but I swear she's still around. You know what I mean? I mean, I can feel her. I've even had a few dreams, and she talks to me, just like you and I are talking."

"I don't think you're crazy at all," she said hoping he didn't think he was either.

"I've heard about that happening to people. When you miss someone a lot, you keep them in your subconscious."

"Do you believe in ghosts?" she asked wondering where the conversation would take them.

Matthew wiped his hands on the napkin on his lap. "If I say yes, are you going to reconsider my verdict of not crazy?"

Grace laughed. "No, because I believe in ghosts. Does that make me crazy?"

His eyes locked with hers. "No. In your line of work, I think deep down inside I personally hope you can see ghosts. Maybe you can even talk to them as they're crossing over. Wow, what a gift that would be."

She couldn't help it. She stared at him, unaware if she were even breathing. Then, she cupped his face with her hands and pressed a hard kiss to his lips.

He jerked from her, and her heart hammered in her chest. What kind of idiot did something like that?

"Sorry. I just…"

Matthew held up his hand. "Don't be sorry. Don't you dare be sorry. It just took me a little by surprise."

He took a deep breath and let it out slowly. "Now, let's try that again."

This time he cupped her face in his hands and pulled her to him. Their lips met softly, and she could feel the warmth that generated between them as they shared the tender moment. She thought he'd pull back again, but instead, he deepened the kiss and her hands came to his chest.

Behind her eyelids, it was as if tiny fireworks lit and exploded. This was going to prove to be a mistake. She didn't care if he said he believed in ghosts. He'd change his mind if she told him what she knew.

But she couldn't pull away. His lips pressed on hers were intoxicating and she was undoubtedly drunk on him.

"This is turning out better than I'd anticipated," he said as he eased back, but his hands remained on her face. "I mean, I'd planned on working into that at some point, but I like having it now even better."

"I'm not usually that forward."

"I didn't think it was too forward."

"Good." She sighed as he dropped his hands. "I don't have too many people that understand me, but you seem to."

"Not to be more forward than we already have been, but I'd like to get to understand you a whole lot more." She watched as his cheeks flushed. "And I don't mean that in a physical term. I mean personally, like maybe we could have lunch tomorrow after I talk to the men at the cemetery."

Deep inside she thought she should decline, play hard to get just a little.

"Let's see how it goes at the cemetery first." Her voice trembled as she spoke. There was a lot of thinking to be had before lunchtime tomorrow, and considering she'd jumped the man and kissed him, she was out of her element.

They continued their dinner seated next to one another sharing the same glass of water. Small talk came naturally, and there were no more mentions about Nora Campbell, though Grace too thought she could feel her close by.

CHAPTER 15

*A*s Matthew drove through the cemetery, he watched as Mr. Rodriguez and Mr. Leeds set up their folding chairs and a small table between them with a cooler at their feet.

A smile came from watching the exchange as he passed toward his grandmother's grave.

He hadn't been there since her funeral a few days earlier, but he felt as though he should have been out there nearly every day since. Life always had a way of getting too busy. He needed to give that more consideration. Maybe he should take more time off and travel more. There was a brand-new mountain bike in his garage that had been precisely ten miles down a path by a creek in town. That was not living.

And wouldn't his grandmother be saddened by the thought that all he did was work? In fact, there he was, in the cemetery to visit because he had a work date.

Well, that was just wrong. He needed to set forth a plan to enjoy the life he'd been given. As he turned the corner, he saw Grace standing over his grandmother's grave with a fistful of daisies. What a picture that made. And just like that, he felt the jolt that slammed into him, and he realized he'd seen that image before in a dream.

Matthew slammed on his brakes before he went off the small path and into a headstone that looked as if it had been standing for decades. He watched as Grace's head popped up at the noise. Crap! he thought as he put the car into park. She certainly was going to believe he was some kind of stalker if he kept looking at her so strangely.

Matthew fixed a smile on his face and climbed from the car with the bouquet he'd brought for his grandmother. "I think these little roads are harder to drive on," he called out to her, and she smiled, thankfully.

She didn't call back to him but continued to smile at him as he walked closer. "Her headstone will be up in a few weeks. The marker doesn't make it look as regal as it will be."

"Regal?"

Grace nodded as she watched him. "You know, more majestic."

"Those are words my grandmother would have chosen for this place."

Grace laughed easily now. "Are they? Well, that's what I think of a headstone. It's a regal marker for someone so important."

Matthew looked across the beautifully manicured acreage scattered with headstones. "There are a lot of important people here," he said, and she lifted her head to take in the scenery too.

"Each and every one of them, important to someone."

He wondered how true that was. Every cemetery had to have someone that had no family, and no one attended their funeral. He found that the very thought made him sadder than finding out his beloved grandmother had passed on.

Clearing his throat, he set the flowers he'd brought next to the marker with his grandmother's name. NORA GRACE CAMPBELL.

"I didn't even think about her middle name being your name."

"She didn't mention that we shared that bond," Grace said and then took a step back. "I mean, I didn't think about it when I saw it on the papers. Of course your grandmother didn't mention it to me." She laughed and then dropped the daisies right next to his flowers and among the arrangements that had been left after the funeral. "I saw the men arrive. Would you like to drive over to them? I saw them setting up."

Matthew looked around the area. "You don't have the cart or your car here?"

"It's a nice walk out here," she said. "We certainly could walk."

Noticing how nervous she was, he thought she could use a walk. "I think the fresh air would do us good."

With a curt nod, Grace took two steps as if to pass him, when she stepped into a divot and propelled herself right into him.

Matthew grabbed her around the waist and stumbled back as she regained her balance in his arms.

"God, I'm such a klutz," she complained with worry masking her face.

"I think it was lucky for me, so don't deny me that," he said, and she laughed.

He didn't let go right away. He found he quite enjoyed her right there in his arms.

"Are you going to let me go?" she finally asked as she smiled up at him.

"I'm not sure I am. Actually, I was just thinking about kissing you again. It's been at least twelve hours since I've done so."

Her cheeks pinked, but she didn't move away. Instead, she lifted her arms around his neck, and he took that kiss he'd been thinking of.

As GRACE EASED BACK, she studied the grin on Matthew's mouth. "I don't make it a point to kiss men I don't know well," she said.

"I guess I'm lucky then."

Lowering her arms and stepping back, Grace brushed her hands over her skirt. "I think we should keep walking."

She watched as he processed her statement with a nod, then motioned for her to lead the way.

They continued through the headstones toward the road where Matthew's car was parked. Perhaps they should take his car, she thought. Then again, when they were done, he could walk one way, and she could walk another. That might be better. Her head was spinning with the what-ifs, and her conscience had a tug-of-war with her body. Kissing the man was lovely, and she'd like to do it a few more times. However, it was inevitable that things would go bad quickly. No man would ever believe she had a to-do list that was given to her by the deceased—especially grandmothers who had recently passed.

"You're walking rather quickly," Matthew said, and Grace slowed as she silently cursed herself. "That's better."

As he caught up to her and walked beside her, she noticed that he had his hands in his pockets. Why wasn't he as frazzled as she was? Did he make it a point to kiss women he didn't know?

The thought only tugged at her more. She was foolish to worry over it. Matthew was in mourning, and people did strange things when they lost a loved one. In all of the pamphlets, they gave to grieving families, one of the first things it said not to do was to make significant, life-changing decisions. Most people made one or two of them in mourning, and how could they not? Between wills, estates, insurance claims, and so many other things, there were a lot of decisions to be made. She knew too that some people sought out the comfort of strangers. Well, she would just assume that was what Matthew was doing by kissing her. It gave him comfort—and she'd admit it gave her comfort too. Not to mention, she'd crossed off a few items from Nora's to-do list, so Grace was going to take that as a win.

"Would you consider having dinner with me next weekend? Socially, not for business like last night," Matthew broke the silence between them without looking at her but continuing to walk with his hands in his pockets.

"You want to see me socially?"

He nodded. "I really would."

"I don't think that's a good idea."

Matthew let out a low hum. "That's disappointing. Maybe I'll ask again another time."

Grace shifted a glance in his direction, but he continued to walk, head up and hands in his pocket. She'd shot him down. He wasn't going to argue?

Perhaps he was more mature than she was. None of this—whatever it was—should matter to her. He was a reporter who needed her help, and she'd obliged. He'd get his stories, and he'd move on. That was how life worked. People were born. People died. People moved on.

As they neared the corner of the two lots, Grace

noticed Mr. Leeds and Mr. Rodriguez settling into their chairs. The sound of the ballgame resonated off of the headstones, and it brought back memories of her own grandfather listening to the games as he worked out in his backyard.

Each of the men stood as they noticed her and Matthew walking toward them.

"Ah, a visitor comes our way," Mr. Leeds laughed. "I have a few more chairs in the car if you'd like to join us."

"What a kind offer," Grace said folding her hands in front of her. "This is Matthew Campbell, and he…"

Mr. Rodriguez pointed a finger at Matthew. "You're on TV. The news," he said.

Matthew smiled. "Yes, sir." He extended his hand. "It's a pleasure to meet you."

Mr. Rodriguez shook his hand. "You just lost your grandmother, right?"

"Yes, sir."

"My condolences. I've been seeing your family come and go the past few days. No loss is easy, but this little lady's family makes it easier."

She caught the admiration in the look that Matthew gave her. "They've been a blessing to my family."

Grace felt her heart rate kick up, and she'd wished she hadn't been so snippy with him on the walk over.

"Mr. Campbell would like to talk to you gentlemen about interviewing you for one of his segments on the news."

Mr. Leeds laughed. "I'm certainly not newsworthy. What could you possibly want to talk to us about?"

"Grace was telling me about the relationship you have formed over the years after your wives passed.

That's of interest to me. I've never known anyone who socially convened in the cemetery before."

"Then you should be here when they have the block party on the other side," he said with a grin.

"I told you," she said to Matthew. "We have quite a community here."

"When do they do their block party?"

The men exchanged glances. "Oh, in the fall I think. And if you're looking at it to take the angle that it's disrespectful, you'll find a fight from us," Mr. Leeds directed to Matthew.

"No, sir. I think that is what community is about. People should come together, no matter where to share."

Mr. Rodriguez stood. "Let me get you two some chairs. We'd love to have you join us for the ballgame and a chat."

CHAPTER 16

The ballgame ended with a home run, and bases loaded in the bottom of the ninth. Matthew couldn't have told anyone who won the game, but the men at the cemetery sure had gotten a kick out of the last-minute rally to take the lead and win the game.

They'd been very cordial, offering him a beer and a chair. They'd talked about their wives, their marriages, and children. Mr. Leeds was Navy, and Mr. Rodriguez was Marine.

Matthew was humbled when Mr. Leeds recalled a few segments he had done on retirement funds and ballot issues in the past election. Mr. Rodriguez let him know he didn't watch TV because he felt it was all trash. He liked his talk radio though, and if Matthew was ever on one of those shows, he ensured him he'd listen.

As Grace and Matthew picked up the chairs they'd been lent, they followed the men to their cars and helped them load back up.

"Well, son, it was a pleasure to meet you. There's a game next Saturday if you want to bring out your camera and talk again. I'm game to be on your TV, even if I'll never see the show," Mr. Rodriguez offered.

Mr. Leeds nodded. "Grace, you come with him. It's been a pleasure to have you spend more time with us. Your family sure helped my family when my wife died. You, in particular, were instrumental in helping my granddaughter cope with the loss of her Mimi."

Grace pressed her hand to her heart and Matthew noticed her eyes had gone moist. "Thank you so very much for that. It means a lot to me. I'll be here."

Pride filled her voice when she spoke, and he knew that even though she'd been born into a family business that most people would find disturbing, Grace Carter took great pride in what she did. All those fancy words she used to describe what her family did weren't just words—they were feelings.

They started back toward his grandmother's grave. Matthew hadn't expected her to head in his direction, but he didn't want to mention it.

"It's interesting to hear that other people have had the same reaction to your family as I have. I thought you were just PC with your words about comfort and how you described the people you work with. But you live and breathe compassion. It flows through your veins, mixed with your blood."

He saw the curve of her lips from the corner of his eye. "That is very sweet of you to say. I believe in the work I do."

"It shows."

They walked the rest of the way in silence until they reached his car and that was when Grace turned to him. "Are you busy now? I mean, do you have somewhere you need to be?"

"No," he said quickly so she would know it was

true. "This, and laundry were the only things on my agenda today."

"Can I take you to lunch? Late lunch I guess since it's nearly three-thirty."

Matthew observed her, noting the well-composed look on her face. "I would like that. Do you want to meet me somewhere? Or I can drive, and I can bring you back to your car."

Again, he marveled at the well-composed Grace as she pondered his offer. "Why don't you drive."

Matthew moved past her and opened the passenger door. Grace slid in with the elegance of a princess and thanked him before he closed the door.

He skirted the front of the car, and as he pulled open the driver's door, he lifted his head as he was sure he'd just heard his grandmother say, "Way to go, champ," just as she once had when he was younger.

"Is everything alright?" Grace asked, and Matthew chuckled.

"Yeah. Just thought I heard something," he offered as he climbed into the car and started the engine.

GRACE HAD HEARD IT. Nora Campbell was reaching out from beyond the grave. Grace folded her hands in her lap and stared forward out the window as Matthew started the car. Was this part of her sixth sense? Had she been able to hear people all along even when they weren't in front of her? Or had she opened up her mind?

As Matthew drove away, she looked out over the headstones. Dear God, were things about to change for her? Would she begin to look in the mirror and see different faces starting back?

She felt the beaded sweat rolled down her back. She didn't want that. Grace had come to terms with the gift, or curse, that she been given at birth. And yes, it did help in the job that she did. She had a little bit of guilt over wearing headphones for so long. But she knew deep down inside she didn't want to carry everybody's last wishes with her. Then there was Nora Campbell. What was it about the woman that made her want to talk to everybody? Why was it now that Grace wanted to hear those last wishes?

Matthew reached across the car and patted her hand. "Are you feeling okay? You seem zoned out."

Grace smiled, with the practiced poise in which she used each day in her work. "I'm fine. I'm sure I'm just hungry. I usually eat lunch around eleven."

Matthew chuckled. "I'm lucky if I even get lunch. I'm usually at the station around six in the morning. You can always guarantee somebody brought a box of donuts if I don't grab something at home. However, if I'm not editing a story, I'm out filming one. People don't think that the special pieces are as intense as heartbreaking news, but the quality ones are."

"The quality comes through," she said honestly. "I look forward to seeing your story on the gentleman and their ballgame."

Matthew smiled. "It'll be a good one, no doubt. I suppose I should consider making it a series. *The other part of death.*" Grace watched as he rubbed his fingers over his chin as if he considered what he was saying. "Yeah, death is inevitable. It's going to happen to every one of us. Some of us are going to get time to say goodbye and get our affairs in order. Others of us are going to go, and no one is prepared. People like you and your family, they help the ones left process it. I could do some interviews with people who counsel the mourning."

Grace watched as he tapped his fingers on the

steering wheel. He wasn't conversing with her any-more, she knew. She had seen her brother do the same thing when he would write songs in his teenage years. Thoughts took over the person, and she was amused as she watched.

"Yeah, one segment can be your family, one seg-ment to be the people celebrating life in a cemetery, I can talk to some grief counselors, what else?" He shifted his glance toward her as they stopped at the stop light.

"You're asking me?"

"Yes. What else is there?"

Grace thought for a moment. "Well, I'm not the first person to receive the deceased. You have to figure at some point maybe they were in the hospital. Nurses are amazing. So are doctors. Corners. Morti-cians. Funeral directors. Seriously, there are as many people involved in death as there are in life."

She thought he would laugh at that, but he didn't. Instead, he continued to drive when the light turned green and was silent for a few more moments.

"Will you help me with this?"

"Me? You want me to help you with your story? For TV?"

"Oh, this has Emmy written all over it. I'll bet no-body knows people throw celebrations at the cemetery."

As Matthew pulled up in front of a Denny's and parked the car, Grace wondered if Nora Campbell had put some of these thoughts into his head. But she had to admit it did have a specific angle for a story. Perhaps she was so caught up in her own world, she didn't realize people didn't know what happened after someone died. Everyone just went through the motions.

"I don't know much how much help I will be. But

it sounds like an adventure. I'll help you as much as I can."

In what must have been sheer excitement, he leaned across the car and kissed her loudly on the lips.

"Thank you. And I'm sorry about the kiss."

"Well, that would be our third kiss. That's something new for me after having only known somebody for a week."

"Me too," he offered, but she wondered how sincere that was. Were men really like that?

"Before we go inside, can I ask you something?"

"Anything."

"You had said you wanted to see me socially. Is that why you want me to work with you on the story?"

Matthew locked his eyes with hers. "I want you to help me with the story because you have a great understanding of the subject matter. You have connections. You have knowledge that I can't even imagine having. And you have the compassion I want to bring to my viewers. As for getting to know you socially, this would only be a bonus. And if you don't want to see me socially, I understand. I won't pursue it. But I would still like your help."

"I'm not good around living. You have to understand that all of my conversations are one-sided."

He smiled at that. "I doubt that. Something tells me you have worked around the deceased long enough that you know what they would say back. And mind you, I think that would be an interesting twist."

Grace's heart began to beat harder. "And what does that mean?"

"I mean, it would be interesting. If the deceased could really talk, what would they say?" His eyes grew wide. "Now not only would that be a great story, but that would make a great book."

"You believe there are people out there like that? People that can talk to the dead?"

"I have never known anyone who admitted that they could. Though, if anyone could, I would think my grandmother could."

Grace's mouth went dry. "And why would you say that?"

"She just had a way about her." He raked his fingers through his hair. "I don't know how to explain it. She just seemed to be more in touch with things than anyone else. Death didn't bother her. Living didn't bother either. I don't think she ever met anyone she didn't like."

Grace thought about the neighbor that had come to Nora's viewing. She wasn't sure Nora cared much for that woman, or for Rebecca Barnes, but then again no one would like everyone.

"The people I work with don't sit up and talk. You know that, right?" she asked as her hands began to shake.

"I don't mean they get up and have a conversation. I mean, it would be cool if you could hear what they were saying." He let out a long breath. "I'm going to be totally honest with you. Back at the cemetery, I thought I heard my grandmother speak to me." He held up his hand. "I know. I know. It sounds crazy, but I did. I'm sure I was worked up over everything."

Grace only nodded. She wasn't ready to tell him her truths yet. She hadn't even known him a week, and she'd already kissed him multiple times and had decided that was going to continue. And, now as she sat in his car, she wondered how long she would hold out the truth that she'd talked to his grandmother.

Matthew opened his door and stepped out of the

car, then ducked to look back inside. "Are you okay? You've gone pale."

Grace batted her eyes and smiled. "I'm fine. I'm hungry."

"A big stack of pancakes is calling my name. And pancakes are good for late lunch," he joked. "C'mon."

CHAPTER 17

*G*race wrapped her hands around the coffee mug and stared out her kitchen window. She hadn't slept well, but that was because her mind was working overtime.

She'd had a wonderful meal with Matthew, in which they held hands across the table while they shared a piece of chocolate pie. He'd driven her back to her car and kissed her goodbye before she'd driven away. God, she was dating a man she didn't even know, and every time she thought about him, her insides turned to jelly.

In the window, she caught the smile that had slipped onto her lips. She looked at the clock on the microwave noting that the morning news had just started.

With her mug of coffee still in her hands, she headed back to her bedroom to turn on the TV and get ready for the day. She had heard from her father, before she turned in for the night, that they had a full docket for the week. They had two new arrivals over the weekend from the hospice by the hospital, and another young cancer patient. There were two viewings and three funerals for the week as well.

To anyone else, the week would sound pathetically sad. To Grace, it was normal. Her life was filled with final goodbyes, and she didn't cry at funerals, only at Nora's.

Grace blew out a breath as she picked up the remote to the TV and turned on the news. She didn't recognize the anchor people sitting behind the big desk. She didn't watch that much TV because it was much too depressing. That thought made her chuckle as she lifted her mug to her lips to sip her coffee. She worked in a funeral home, and the news was depressing.

"Coming up in ten, our own Matthew Campbell is live from the riverfront where they are already getting set up for the upcoming Fourth of July festivities."

Grace walked into her bathroom and picked up the brush off the counter before walking back to the bedroom and sitting on the bed. She set her coffee on the nightstand and began to brush her hair as she watched endless commercials about furniture and car sales.

The Fourth of July was one of Grace's favorite holidays. Picnics by the river with fireworks after. Her family had always made it a family event which she looked forward to. Had it been a tradition for the Campbell family too? Was it possible she had crossed paths with Nora Campbell and her grandson multiple times in the past?

"Good morning, I'm Matthew Campbell live this morning from River Front Park."

She lifted her head when she heard his voice on the TV. The tumble her heart took when she saw him with the microphone in front of him was something she hadn't expected. Oh, she loved looking at him, and the kisses they'd shared were delightful, but this was something else.

She held the brush in her hand as she watched Matthew on TV showing the viewers the set up for the festivities. There was something more between them—more than even she wanted to admit to. Had Nora Campbell coordinated this in life and acted on it in death? And why Grace? Why would Nora choose her, someone she'd never met, over a world of other people?

"Festivities for Fourth of July kick off at three o'clock with live music, dancing, and food. I've been told that this year's fireworks display will put all other displays to shame." The laughter lit in his voice and squeezed at Grace's heart.

"Matthew, what are you wearing?" The anchor-woman asked as she squinted her eyes as if she were looking at the monitor across the room. "Do you have on a bumble bee pin?"

Grace stood from her bed and moved to the TV.

Matthew laughed as he tapped the pin that was right next to his channel four pin on his shirt. "I do. You know that bumblebees aren't supposed to be able to fly, but they do. It's a symbol of strength that my grandmother used to wear, and I thought it was appropriate today. She was a great lover of this River Front Park tradition."

"Thanks, Matthew. We always learn something new from you," the anchorwoman said as the screen went back to just those in the studio now reporting about an overturned truck on the highway.

Grace turned off the TV and then noticed her bumble bee pin laying on the dresser next to the TV.

She picked it up and smiled down at it. She thought she'd lost it, but she was sure she hadn't set it on the dresser. It wasn't on her dress when she'd taken it off.

That moment she smelled the faint smell of roses and moved to the window. The bush in her tiny backyard was in full bloom. Opening the window, she took in a deep breath and the air was filled with the scent that lifted from the bush.

"Oh, Nora, are you gardening from the other side now?" she asked aloud thinking of the woman and her rose bushes. "That bush has never bloomed like that."

The TV turned back on, and Matthew's segment started over. Grace turned to watch, and the scent of roses grew heavier.

She knew that Nora Campbell was with her in that room even if she couldn't see her or hear her. And even though she had the gift to talk to the other side, it should have made her a little frightened to smell that scent and to have her TV turning on to something that had already played. But instead, she found comfort in knowing Nora was around.

"The fireworks are my favorite," Grace said as she turned off the TV again. "My family goes every year and picnics. I was thinking of asking Matthew to join us," she offered as a breeze past through the room, and then the rose scent was gone.

"Well, I'm going to assume that was what she wanted me to say." Grace opened her hand and looked down at the bumblebee pin. She wondered how it would compare to Nora's. Perhaps she'd ask Matthew to show it to her.

Grace tucked the pin into her jewelry box and then went back into the bathroom to style her hair and get ready for work.

Before she left for work, she poured herself another cup of coffee in her favorite travel mug, grabbed a banana, tucked it into her bag, and then picked up her purse. As she headed for the door, she backed up when she noticed that the drawer to her desk in the living room was wide open.

Grace's spine stiffened as she looked around the small townhouse. Nothing else in the entire house was out of place.

Slowly, she walked toward the drawer and saw the book where she'd long ago tucked away the list from Mrs. Rodriguez and the combination from Mr. Jackson laying at the top of the drawer.

With an unsteady hand, she picked up the book and again smelled the faint scent of roses.

"You want me to attend to these? It's been years," she said aloud with no response. "People are going to think I'm crazy."

She set the book back in the drawer and closed it. But as she turned around, she heard it slide open again.

Okay, if Nora Campbell was going to haunt her forever, they were going to need to set down some ground rules.

Grace turned back and picked up the book. "I will take it with me and see what I can do. But that's it. From now on, I'm going into the room with my headphones on. I can't take on everyone's last wishes."

The scent of roses spiraled around her and then faded away.

CHAPTER 18

$\mathcal{T}$he red book under Grace's arm was heavy, which was stupid because it wasn't a heavy book. As she pushed open the door to the mortuary, her mother was the first person she saw.

"Oh, good. You're here," her mother said as she hurried toward her. "Juan is done with one of the women who came in from the hospice this weekend. Mrs. Jones needs to be tended to first because her family wants to do a funeral here and then they are going to take her to Nebraska for final resting. But we have to move quickly there."

Her mother handed her the file on Mrs. Jones.

"Ms. Cartwright is the other from the hospice, and her daughter is in the family waiting room. She would like to discuss plans with you."

"Me?"

"For how she wants her to look."

Grace's breath caught in her lungs. She didn't meet with the family, usually. This wasn't how she wanted to start her morning.

"Can't someone else meet with her? I don't do this part."

"You'll be fine. Your father and your brother are

working with three other families. It was a busy weekend."

Her mother handed her the file on Ms. Cartwright and turned and walked away.

Taking a deep breath, Grace headed to the family room without even dropping her items in the employee lounge.

Ms. Cartwright's daughter sat at the table. She couldn't have been older than thirty but trapped in the hippy culture of the 1960s. The white cotton dress she wore had a crocheted neckline, and she actually wore a beaded headband across her forehead and over her straight, long brown hair.

When the woman saw Grace, she stood and moved to her enveloping her in a hug.

"Hello, sister. I'm so happy you're here," she offered as a welcome in Grace's ear.

"Hello," Grace managed as the woman stepped aside.

"I am Beth Cartwright. I'm told you will be working on my mother."

"Grace Carter," she offered as she set her items on the table in the room and held out her hand to shake Beth's.

Beth shook her head and pulled Grace in for another hug. "Handshakes are impersonal."

When Beth stepped back, Grace quickly motioned to the chair. "Have a seat, and we can go over plans for your mother."

Because it was the protocol to sit near the family, an intimate gesture, Grace had done so. However, when Beth took her hand and held it in hers, she wished she'd thought more about protocol.

"Sister Grace, my mother's wishes were to die peacefully in her sleep, and my guilt floods me that she died in a hospice on morphine."

"Hospice care is offered so that passing is painless."

"Yes, and for her it was. And the staff there were so sweet and wonderful. None of them were connected though, do you know what I mean?"

"Not exactly."

Beth smiled sweetly at Grace. "I mean no one could talk to her when her spirit passed before her body did. And I know she has more to say."

Panic lodged itself in Grace's throat like a stone. "I'm sure they did all they could for her."

"Yes, of course. But I would like you to ask her what she would like me to do for her. We are not traditional, as you might have noticed. I'm not sure my mother would want to be embalmed and put in the ground. However, before my father passed, he made plans for both of them to be buried together. I think that was the right choice for him, but not for her."

"And you want me to ask her?"

"I do."

"And what makes you think that she will answer me?"

Beth's lips parted in a wide smile. "I heard a voice last night when my mother passed that said *Grace would know. Grace would ask.* Imagine my surprise when I arrived this morning and learned that there was a Grace."

Grace's palms had gone damp. "Someone told you I would talk to your mother?"

"Yes. I know that I've met you, I know that's true. I feel the vibrations in you. Whoever came to me brought with them the scent of roses."

Grace pulled back her hand. "Would you excuse me for a moment?"

She stood from the table, leaving all of her personal items in the room, and marched down the hallway to the room with Ms. Cartwright's name on the door."

Just as she might have once done to her brother, she burst into the room. "What are you doing?"

Ms. Cartwright lay on the table, draped and cleaned just as Grace would have expected her to be. She too was much younger than Grace had assumed she would be.

"Welcome, sister Grace."

"Ms. Cartwright?"

"Sylvia, dear. My name is Sylvia."

"Hello, Sylvia." Grace fisted her hands to her side. "Do you have Nora Campbell with you."

There was a light laugh in Grace's ears. "Yes, dear. She is here. She wonders why you didn't wear the bumblebee."

"I forgot it. Would you please ask her to not send people to me to talk to their loved ones."

Sylvia laughed again. "She says it's part of you and your future. It's your calling."

"I don't want to be known as some freak that can talk to the dead."

"Oh, darling. No one thinks that. You offer a service to everyone this way."

"Why does she want me to do this?"

"She doesn't. She's just leading you to your destination."

"And this is my calling? To take the final requests from those who have passed?"

Sylvia was silent for a moment. "She says that and to marry her grandson. She says he loves you."

"I've only started to get to know him," Grace offered. "I don't think we're in love."

"Oh, sister Grace, give it time. He is part of this journey." Grace heard Sylvia whisper to someone, but it was inaudible. "She says she will talk to you later. I, on the other hand, want to tell you what to tell my daughter."

A half hour later, Grace walked through the door to the family room where Beth still sat at the table.

"I'm sorry, I should have offered you something to drink or eat," she said as she shut the door behind her.

"I only eat what I grow. Thank you though. So, what did my mother say?"

Grace sat down next to Beth and looked her in the eyes. The woman was absolutely sure Grace would give her the answers and was okay with how she got the information. Was everyone going to be like this? If Grace told Matthew that she was conversing with his grandmother would he be okay with that or would he run in the opposite direction?

"Your mother doesn't want to be buried."

"I knew it."

"She would like me to make her up for viewing for her family, but then she would like to be cremated and scattered among the daisies."

Beth clasped her hands together and laughed. "I knew that's what she would want. Oh, I'm so happy to know this. I would have been so sad to have placed her in the ground. Did she say anything about my father?"

"Just that he'd agreed with her wishes."

Beth nodded. "Thank you, sister Grace. What you have done, I can never repay." Again, Beth moved in and enveloped Grace in a hug. "I have her clothes in the car and a photo of how she should look for her viewing. You're an angel on earth, sister Grace. May peace always be with you."

Beth excused herself from the room to gather the items she had for Grace.

Alone, Grace contemplated what had just happened. Her gift had always been her own secret, but now she had a spirit on the other side offering her up. Was that what she really wanted to do? Would it give others peace?

The scent of roses filled the air, and Grace closed her eyes. *One time*, she thought the words clearly. *I did this one time. I don't know that I can do it all the time.*

The rose scent grew stronger, and she was quite sure she'd been kissed on the cheek.

CHAPTER 19

*M*onday quickly slipped into Tuesday. Grace had forgone the headphones, though she had made that clear to Nora that she wouldn't be willfully talking to anyone else.

Now her mind raced with the last wishes of Sylvia Cartwright, the prayer that Mr. Grover wanted to be said at his funeral, and she needed to figure out how to tell Mr. Simon that his wife left six thousand dollars in a shoe box in the discarded Christmas decorations box in their crawl space.

As she worked on a very quiet Mr. Kurtz, she smelled the roses before she heard the man's voice. "I'm supposed to tell you to open the door."

"I'm working," Grace said, her voice filled with irritation at the slight demand.

When she heard the knocking, she turned and flung open the door.

"Hi," Matthew said standing in the hallway with a bouquet of roses in his hand. "I don't mean to interrupt, but..."

He didn't get any other words out before Grace felt the slap of a hand on her back lunging her through the door and right at him.

"Whoa, are you okay?" he asked as he held her against him.

"Fine."

"I was worried about you. I hadn't heard from you in the past few days, and you didn't return my calls."

"I've been busy," she said as she stood back and tucked her hands into her apron pockets.

"These are for you," he offered as he handed her the roses. "My sister cut them from the bush we planted at her house. Can you believe they look this nice?"

Yes, she could. Whatever powers Nora Campbell had on the other side, it included gardening.

Grace took a moment to smell the scented petals and calm her nerves. "Thank you for thinking of me. I'm sorry I've been M.I.A."

"I get it. Are you free tonight? Can I take you to dinner?"

The voice from the other room echoed in her head. *Tell him yes.*

It was at that moment she decided to close the door.

"I would love to. I'll be done about five, does that work?"

"I'll pick you up then." He leaned in and kissed her on the cheek, then turned to walk away.

She couldn't blame him. Who would want to put up with a moody woman? She was annoying herself at the moment.

"Matthew," she called after him. "Would you like to go with me to the fireworks tomorrow? It's a family tradition to picnic and stay for the show."

A sexy smile formed on his lips. "I'm doing a re-mote segment for the ten o'clock. I'll be there. I'll find you."

She expected he'd keep walking, but was surprised when he turned back, cupped her face in his hands, and lingered a gentle kiss on her lips.

"I'll see you soon," he whispered as he gazed at her, then he strode off down the hall, now with a spring in his step.

Grace opened the door to the room where Mr. Kurtz rested.

"She says her rose bushes look wonderful this year," his voice filled Grace's ears with Nora's words.

"Mr. Kurtz, did you ever garden?"

"No, ma'am. I mowed the lawn. The rest of the yard was my wife's. From the looks of it, she didn't have the same talent as this other woman."

Grace chuckled as she reached for her palette of colors to begin working on Mr. Kurtz. She wondered if it annoyed him to have Nora speak through him. Admittedly, it annoyed her a bit. She was going to keep talking to Nora Campbell, she would like to do it one on one.

"Mr. Kurtz," Grace began as she placed the foundation on his face. "Thank you for being the receptor between Nora Campbell and me. I promise I won't use you much longer for that. Would you just let her know that I'm having dinner with her grandson this evening, and I invited him to fireworks tomorrow? That should be all for now."

She heard a sound as if Mr. Kurtz were clearing his throat, and she found that odd.

"She said she'd be quiet, but she wants to make sure you have the book from the desk."

Grace looked down at Mr. Kurtz, and she smiled as if he were going to open his eyes and look about her, but he didn't of course. "I have it, and I will attend to it."

"She says okay, and now she's not here."

Grace knew that too. She could always feel the void when Nora Campbell moved on.

Nora must've made Mr. Kurtz pretty nervous because once she left, he was free to talk himself. He didn't have any last wishes, and he felt he had a full life. The entire time Grace worked on him, he told her of his work, his time in the Army, his wife, and their six grandkids. She gathered he wasn't too proud of his son and daughter, they seem to have each had a different path in life than the one he would have chosen for them, but he did love his grandchildren.

"All done," Grace said as she stepped back and looked down at Mr. Kurtz. "Very handsome."

"Ninety-four. No one is handsome at ninety-four."

Grace laughed. "Well, consider yourself the first then. I think your family will be happy with how you look."

"I lived a lot of days. I never thought I wanted to see the other side. I fought long and hard not to. But that lady that was here, she makes it seem okay. I think it'll be all right."

Grace felt the pressure in her chest. Nora was like a welcoming party on the other end. A part of her wished she had known the woman in life.

Grace turned at the tapping at the door just as her brother opened it. "We are ready to dress him now."

"He is ready," Grace said as she gathered her tools and sponges for cleaning.

"Where did the roses come from?" Scott asked.

"Nora Campbell's grandson brought them. They are off of one of her rose bushes."

He gave a low hum. "Mama said you met him for dinner the other night."

"It was a business meeting. He wants to do a news piece on the men in the cemetery. So, we met with them, listened to a baseball game, and next week he's going to come and video. He wants to do a segment on the big block party next time too."

"Bring on the mariachi."

Grace laughed as she put her brushes and tools in the sanitizing jar. "Are you afraid of death?" she asked her brother as he unzipped the garment bag with Mr. Kurtz's clothing.

Scott shrugged. "I'm not afraid of it. I mean, it's going to happen, and I won't know it. I think I would like to be old, like Mr. Kurtz. But I sure as hell don't want you to put makeup on me."

That time Grace snorted out a laugh. "Are you afraid I would use the wrong color lipstick?"

Scott rolled his eyes. "I'm afraid you would take liberty with everything. As far as I'm concerned, cremate me and scatter me throughout the cemetery. Hopefully, by the time I go, the people I love and will be here, and I can be with them."

"But you're not afraid?"

Scott lifted his eyes and looked at her sincerely. "No, I'm not afraid. And I know, if I go before you do, I'll still get to you." He gave her a wink and went back to his work.

Grace stood there for another moment. Though her brother teased her often about talking to herself, he accepted the gift she was given. Was that weird to him? Did he possess some sort of gift to?

Now wasn't the time to ask, she decided as she watched her brother begin to dress Mr. Kurtz.

Grace picked up the small bouquet of roses and carried them in the crook of her arm out of the room. Her brother's words were still echoing in her ears. It gave him comfort to know that he could still talk to her even in death. Did she offer comfort to those who pass by giving them that gift to? Was that her true calling?

She walked to the employee lounge and opened up her locker. Inside was the book that she had brought from home on Nora's suggestion.

She pulled it from the locker and set it on the table with the roses. Flipping open the page, she looked down at the list that Mrs. Rodriguez had given her. Some of the items, Grace knew, had already been checked off. Not because she had been any help in it, but there were a few that still needed to be tended to.

And then there was Mr. Jackson's safe combination. Grace shook her head as she held the small piece of paper in her hand. She would have to give that some thought. How did you approach a widow with such a strange artifact?

The scent of roses grew more substantial, and Grace knew it wasn't just the bouquet that sat next to her. "I will check these items off the list. And I will get this combination to his wife," she promised. "I don't know how long I can do this. Someone is bound to think I'm after something, and that's not true."

She ran her fingers over the list and thought about the day that she had written it. Mrs. Rodriguez was young, her life stolen by cancer. Was she at peace now? Or was she waiting for Grace to finish her work?

"Matthew is going to think I'm crazy if I tell him this."

There were no words, and nothing in the room was disturbed, but she felt Nora Campbell's retort in her heart.

"I'll tell him. But if he walks away and thinks I'm crazy, the headphones go back on. He's very open-minded, and if this is something he's not open-minded to then the rest of the world won't be either."

She felt the rose-scented breeze whip around her as if in an embrace before it disappeared.

Looking down at the list and the combination, Grace closed her eyes and took a deep breath. Nora Campbell had led her to her calling, and now it seemed that Grace was in the business of granting last goodbyes.

CHAPTER 20

*L*aughter came from the lobby, and that wasn't a natural sound. But it was Ella's laugh, and that carried a mighty boom.

Grace knew there were no families in the building, or Ella would never be so careless. As she walked toward the front of the building, she heard the familiar voice that was kickstarted her heart rate every time she heard it.

"And the man began throwing eggs at us to get us off of his street corner," Matthew said, and Ella roared in laughter again, fanning herself with a pamphlet.

"Oh, Grace, this guy is a hoot."

Grace exchanged glances with Matthew. "I haven't seen that side yet," she admitted. "What is he telling you?"

Matthew gave her a wink. "Just some funny in-the-field stories. Are you ready to go?"

"I am." Grace turned to Ella. "What are your plans for tomorrow?"

"My grandson wants to set off fireworks. He's eight," she directed toward Matthew. "I'm afraid he might be a bit of a pyromaniac. I'm trying to decide how I want to handle this."

Matthew smiled at her. "The fireworks down by the river are always nice."

Ella puckered her lips and gave it some thought. "I wonder if I could bribe him with carnival rides and food," she contemplated. "I'm going to try that."

"Well I hope we see you there," Matthew said as he slipped his hand onto the small of Grace's back and it sent a tingle up her spine. "My car is just out front."

Grace walked toward the front door, which Matthew pulled open for her. She could feel the admiring stare from Ella, but she didn't turn back around to acknowledge it.

His hand returned to her back as they walked toward his car. "Ella isn't an easy one to win over. How did you manage that?"

"Why do you say she's not easy to win over? She smiled the moment I walked in. She laughed at my very first joke. She asked where I was taking you because she cares for you."

"She's like a second mother. I've known her my whole life."

"I have a feeling if I'm going to keep seeing you, I'm going to have to prove my worth to a lot of people."

She laughed easily as she climbed into the car. "Not that many, I'm sure."

Matthew shut the door, and walked around to the other side, then climbed in. "Do you like sushi?"

Grace gave it a moment of thought. "I have only had California rolls at the grocery store. Is that considered sushi?"

Matthew chuckled as he started the engine. "It is. There are a lot of varieties. You don't have to eat the raw stuff."

"Give me an example."

Matthew put the car in reverse and backed out of the parking space. "Shrimp tempura roles are my mother's favorite. In fact, if you ever eat sushi with her, don't eat her roles. Just a warning. I've been stabbed with many a chopstick."

"I promise to never do that," she said as she laughed, and he merged onto the street. "I'm game. But here's the deal. If I don't like it, you'll have to get me a cheeseburger."

Matthew took one of his hands off the steering wheel and reached across to grab hers. He interlaced their fingers. "That's a promise I can make."

Grace looked down at their hands. There was comfort there.

When should she tell him about the conversations she had had with his grandmother? Over dinner? Or should she wait until they got back to the mortuary and at least she had her own car?

Matthew gave her hand a squeeze. "Got something on your mind today?"

Grace chewed her bottom lip for a moment. "Yes."

"Would you like to talk about it?"

She turned her gaze to look at him. "Yes, I do. I'm just not sure if I can wrap my own head around it, let alone share it with you."

"Why can't you share with me?"

"Well, I've known you exactly one week. You're in a state of mourning."

"And you don't think we should be starting a relationship."

"Let's just say I've always been warned against such a thing."

Matthew nodded slowly as he pulled to a stop light. "Have you had a lot of family members of the deceased that you work with want to date you?"

Grace shook her head. "No. I've never let myself get into a situation like this."

Matthew looked up at the light and slowly eased forward as it turned green. "So, I should be a little bit flattered? I mean I'm the first guy, ever, that has been forward enough to ask you out? Good for me."

He had a way of easing the situation. Was he as trained as she was? After all, he had to convince people to talk to him and let him video them for TV.

"I did have a man asked me out once," she reminisced. "I was probably twenty, and he was probably fifty. It was during his sister's service, and I remember that they were a very dysfunctional family."

"I'm picturing one of those old uncles, beer belly, unshaven, suit coat that won't button."

Again, she laughed easily and was delighted to do so. "That's exactly what he was like. I'm disgusted by it even now."

"In a roundabout way, you're saying I'm good-looking?"

She turned to stare at him, as he pulled into the parking lot of the restaurant. "I do think you're handsome."

"Good. I think you're beautiful."

Matthew put the car in park and turned off the engine. Grace sat there, her eyes still locked on his face.

"Is this weird? I'm so comfortable with you, and you make me laugh. I keep coming up with reasons that I shouldn't continue to see you. You know, reasons that I associate with my job. Perhaps, when your life moves on comfortably without your grandmother, I won't be important anymore."

He turned fully toward her holding both of her hands in his. "I'm not the kind of guy who doesn't take relationships seriously. If I start a relationship with someone, I wanted to work out. If something goes horribly wrong, I don't want that person to hate me, so I eased out of it, with full disclosure. I like you, Grace. I'd like to think that this relationship would work out for the long haul."

"And what about Rebecca Barnes?"

His eyes opened wide, and he sat back a bit. "Rebecca Barnes? You're asking me about Rebecca Barnes?"

"I know that she's very interested in you."

"And has been since high school. I am not interested in her. I think I made that clear at my grandmother's viewing."

Grace considered that, but she had facts. "She spent the night at your house."

Now his brows drew together. "How did you know that?"

"You wouldn't believe me if I told you."

"Try me," he said, but his voice had gone flat.

"I think I'd rather try sushi first." She looked at their hands, their fingers intertwined, and took a breath. "She's not part of your life like that?"

"I'm not sure how much clearer I can make that."

Grace pulled her hands from his and placed them on his cheeks. "I don't play the field."

"Neither do I."

"I believe you," she said as she pressed a kiss to his lips that sizzled.

The air in the car grew even hotter as Matthew pulled Grace closer to him and deepened the kiss.

Her head swam with vibrant color, and the breath in her lungs grew heavier. If her heart slammed any harder against her ribs, it would break free from her chest.

"Well," he said as he caught his breath. "That

worked up my appetite. Are we good here?" He asked sucking in another breath.

Grace nodded.

"Who told you about Rebecca?"

"I'll tell you when we get back to the mortuary. I want to enjoy my evening with my boyfriend," she offered with a smile.

Matthew puckered his lips. "I like that word. Sounds innocent."

"We are."

He nipped her lips with his again. "For now, we most certainly are."

CHAPTER 21

A true gentleman, that was what Matthew Campbell was. Not once had he brought up the subject of how Grace knew about Rebecca Barnes, just as she'd asked him not to.

During dinner, he utilized the opportunity for them to get to know each other away from their work.

Matthew had been an all-state baseball player and a track star. His athleticism had paid his way through college on scholarships. He'd been in a fraternity his freshman year, and then did not return to it his sophomore year, "because some things are more important than parties and girls."

Right there she'd felt her heart tumble. He was everything she'd hoped he'd be.

Matthew didn't seem too surprised when Grace told him she'd been timid throughout high school. She was in choir and did anything backstage in a theater, but certainly didn't want to be front and center. College had never been in her plans, but trade school had. She'd dreamed of being a hairstylist her entire life, and when she told him that, he hadn't flinched or laughed. Instead, he'd made some comment about how useful it was as a career and how everyone needed a hairstylist, even when they were down on their luck. Usually, the first person people called was their stylist to make them feel good again or to look good to land a job.

And just like that, her heart tumbled even more.

Grace found that she did enjoy sushi, though she stayed with the cooked pieces. They'd had a small bottle of sake, and she was glad that it would wear off before she had to drive home.

They filled two hours with conversation ranging from Christmas traditions to favorite Happy Meal toys as a child. Grace was sure there was nothing left that she didn't know about Matthew Campbell.

She basked in the feeling of being full, both figuratively and spiritually as they drove back to the mortuary holding hands.

"All talked out? You're awfully quiet over there," Matthew said, and Grace rolled her head to the side to look at him.

"I was just thinking how full I was. Both my belly and my soul."

He lifted her hand to his lips and pressed a kiss to her fingers. "I feel the same way. I'm going to go into work early tomorrow and get everything set up for this weekend so that we can shoot the piece on the gentlemen in the cemetery."

"You don't get tomorrow off at all?"

"News never takes a break. Not even the good news stuff. What about you?"

"It's one of the days we, as a family, take off. Everyone else on staff usually takes a holiday to be on call. We still receive people, but we don't do anything else."

"I assume Christmas and Thanksgiving are the only other days when you have some peace?"

"Yes. Life starts and ends on its own time, and it doesn't wait for weekends and holidays."

The parking lot was empty when they arrived back at the mortuary. Matthew pulled up next to Grace's car and shut off the engine.

Neither of them moved.

"I had a wonderful night," she said looking down at their hands that were still entwined.

"I did too. I'm hesitant to let it end. But…"

Grace sighed. This was as far as it could go right now. Relationship or not, she wasn't ready to take him home or go home with him. Then again, he didn't ask either.

"I guess I'll see you tomorrow. I'll save room on my blanket for you, and some of mom's apple pie. You'll want that."

"I'd never turn down apple pie," he said as he ran his thumb over her fingers. "But don't we have one more conversation?"

Grace bit the inside of her cheek. There was a part of her that had hoped he'd forgotten. But it was an excellent time to get it out in the open.

"Right."

"So, who told you that Rebecca Barnes spent the night?"

MATTHEW WATCHED Grace shifted her seat. He wasn't pleased that someone had told her that Rebecca had spent the night, but then he wasn't sure who even knew besides him and Rebecca. Anger lit inside of him wondering if it had been Rebecca. He wouldn't put it past her. He had been flirty with Grace, and he'd done it on purpose. Well, and he quite enjoyed it. But it would be just like Rebecca to do something like stirring the pot, to try and cause trouble.

He was ready to pull his phone out of his pocket and call Rebecca when Grace took a breath.

"Your grandmother," she said as she squeezed her eyes shut.

Matthew sat there for a moment, perhaps shocked and silenced by her answer. Had she really just said his grandmother told her that? Was this some kind of joke?

This wasn't funny, and no matter how attracted to her, or how good he felt around her, he wasn't going to take this.

Matthew opened his car door and hurried around to the other side as Grace opened hers.

"Forget it. I'm sorry I said anything." Grace grabbed her purse out of the car and shoved past him.

He watched her tear through her purse for her keys, her hands shook, and he could hear the sobbing. Seriously, if someone were trying to hurt him, why would they be crying that much?

Grace pulled her keys from her purse with such force that they flew from her fingers and under the car. She stomped her foot and dropped her purse on the ground.

Wiping at her face to brush away the tears, Grace knelt down next to her car.

Matthew watched the episode unfold in front of him. She was absolutely distraught, and he was just standing there.

"When was that?" he asked because all of a sudden he truly believed maybe his grandmother had talked to her.

"Never mind. I saw how you looked at me. You

don't believe me. I don't expect you to believe me. And..." She stopped speaking and sat back on her heels letting the tears roll down her cheeks.

"I'm just a little shocked by your answer, that's all."

"I know, it sounds crazy. But it's the truth. She was very upset about it."

Matthew closed his eyes tightly now and pressed his fingers to them. He swore he was nearly dizzy with the scent of roses spinning around him. Opening his eyes, he knelt down next to Grace.

"When did she tell you this?"

Grace blew out a breath and turned to look at him through tear filled eyes. "At her funeral."

Matthew sat flat on the pavement. Now he knew he was dizzy on the scent of roses. His breath hurt in his lungs, and it took everything he could to push it out. "My grandmother spoke to you at her funeral?"

He noticed the tears had stopped in Grace's eyes, and now a fire lit behind them. "I'm telling you the truth. And this is who I am. And if you don't like it, you can..."

Matthew reached for her arm as she started to stand and pulled her down next to him. She landed with an *umph* on her ass, but he could tell it hadn't hurt, so he wasn't going to fuss over it.

"Shut up for a minute," he said perhaps a little too forcefully. "Give me a damn minute to wrap my head around this."

He pressed his fingers to his temple and closed his eyes again.

"God, I swear somebody just sprayed rose perfume or something. I actually think I'm going to get sick from the scent," he said, and then he heard Grace laugh. "You're laughing at me?"

"At this point, you think I'm crazy anyway. But

when your grandmother is around, she smells like roses."

He stared at her blankly. "My grandmother is here?"

"I guess so, you can smell her."

"Fine. What does she say about this?"

"Here's the deal, I can only talk to someone from the other side when I am with them. When they are laying on my table, or in their casket, I can hear them." Grace dropped her shoulders and fold her hands in her lap. "I have a combination to a safe from six years ago. I have an entire list of things that Mrs. Rodriguez wanted to have done that she never got to do. Your grandmother wanted your sister to have that rosebush, and she told me where the key was for the lockbox."

Matthew rocked back-and-forth slowly thinking about the things that happened days after his grand-mother had passed. "You are the one that suggested the rosebush go to my sister."

"It was what your grandmother wanted."

"You told me we would find the key to the lockbox between the mattress and the box springs."

"Because that's where she told me it was."

Matthew winced. "She knew Rebecca Barnes spent the night at my house?"

"Yes. She was quite distraught about it the morning of her funeral." She stopped and smiled. "She was arguing with me about it when you came up and asked if I always talked to the plants."

"You were talking to my grandmother?"

"Yes. And at that moment you touched my arm and spoke to me very softly. When you walked away, Nora began to laugh. Then she said she had nothing to worry about. Rebecca Barnes wasn't a problem.

She saw how you'd looked at me, and then she said she was ready to go."

"That's a lot to take in."

"So maybe you should go home and reconsider everything I told you. She's been very adamant that I give last goodbyes since I can. The other day I gave two little girls a message that their mother gave to me. I put a certain color lipstick on a woman whose daughter-in-law wiped it off, but I'll be damned if she wasn't buried in the color she wanted. I don't know that I have it in me to grant these last wishes. But it's what she wants me to do."

"You've talked to her more than just while she was with you, haven't you?"

Grace chuckled. "I've never had anyone else do this, but your grandmother will come through when I'm with somebody else. I don't hear her voice, but she talks to them, and they talk to me. However," she began as she brushed the dirt from her skirt, "that bumblebee pin I thought I had lost appeared the other morning during your newscast, while I was watching it. It was sitting right on my dresser, and I know it wasn't there before. Then, when I went downstairs, the desk drawer where I kept the notes from Mrs. Rodriguez was open. After I closed it and turned around, it was open again."

"My grandmother?"

"Scent of roses everywhere."

"If anyone in this universe, or any universe, could get through to somebody, it would be her."

"So you believe me?"

"I want to," he said reaching for her hand.

"It's a little unorthodox, and no one can know about it, but I can prove it to you."

"How?"

143

"Let's go inside. Mr. Kurtz's funeral is on Thursday. He can help us."

Matthew felt the blood drain from his face. "We're going to go inside and talk to a dead guy?"

"He is deceased," she corrected his wording. "However, he is prepared. But your grandmother will talk to me through him. It's the only we can prove this to you."

Matthew swallowed hard and rose to his feet. He reached his hand to Grace, who scrambled for her car key before he helped her up.

"I've done a lot of crazy things to get a good story. This is got to be the craziest thing I've ever done."

"Don't do it unless you trust me."

Matthew raised his hand to her cheek and caressed it with his thumb. "The craziest thing in the world is that I trust you more than I've ever trusted anyone."

"Good. Because I think your grandmother trusts me too."

Grace slipped her hand into his as they walked toward the building, which had been dark, but now lights turned on.

"Who's in there?" he asked.

"No one."

"She's turning on the lights?"

"I have to assume so."

He felt his body begin to shake with nerves and then felt foolish about it. This was his grandmother after all.

"I thought I heard her in the cemetery the other day after I'd asked you out again."

Grace smiled up at him. "I have no doubt you did."

Just as she slipped the key into the lock, Matthew turned her toward him. "Rebecca spent the night that night," he admitted and felt her stiffen under his touch. "But we only slept. I've never let our relationship go further than that. I just wanted you and her," he turned toward the door, "to know that. It's important that you do know that."

Grace's smile widened. "I appreciate that. Now, c'mon. I'm sure your grandmother is anxious to talk to you."

CHAPTER 22

*M*atthew tucked his hands into his pockets since they wouldn't stop shaking. A million different thoughts ran through his head as he followed Grace into the mortuary.

What if she were some kind of serial killer? How had his grandmother really turned on all those lights? What was he going to wear to the fireworks tomorrow night?

Pulling one shaky hand from his pocket, he ran it through his hair. "I don't know why I'm so nervous. I didn't think I was crazy when I heard her voice in the cemetery, but now I think I'm certifiable."

He heard Grace chuckle as she stopped in the hallway. "Second door on your left is the employee lounge. There's a fantastic espresso machine in there and a refrigerator full of soda, water, and juices. Why don't you go in, sit down, and have something to drink. I'm going to go get Mr. Kurtz prepared, and then we can visit with him."

"You're going to prepare him? You don't trust me to just walk into a room and open casket?"

Grace reached her hand out to his, and the warmth of her touched eased his nerves. "You're a newsman. I'm sure you can handle that just fine. I am offering the man I'm using some dignity. Even in death, people deserve to be treated well."

Matthew let out a slow breath. And here he'd thought she might be a serial killer.

"Okay. I will go get something to drink and wait for you."

She smiled at him as she let go of his hand. He could feel her gaze on him as he walked away and entered the lounge.

Just as Grace had said, the refrigerator was full of bottled drinks. He chose a bottle of orange juice, and then returned it for a bottle of water. His stomach already turned with nerves at the thought of talking to his grandmother.

He tried to wrap his head around the gift he was being given. No one usually got the chance to speak to somebody after they had passed, but he was going to. All of a sudden, he couldn't think of a thing to ask his grandmother. Maybe he didn't want to talk to her. What he really wanted to do was hug her.

Tears welled in his eyes and laughter bubbled in his chest. It was crazy that he was this nervous.

Matthew opened the bottle of water and took a long drink.

When the door opened behind him, he turned to see Grace standing there. "We are ready. Are you?"

"I have never been so freaked out in my life," he said, unsure of why.

"I would totally understand if you don't want to go through with this."

Matthew secured the top on the bottle and set it on the table. He walked to her and placed his hands on her arms. Looking down into her dark eyes, he felt a calm that he hadn't felt in a very long time.

"I need to go through this. I need to know what

you told me is absolutely the truth, though I can't imagine you would ever lie. You're not that kind of person. It's just a lot to wrap my head around."

"I've never done this for anyone else, Matthew. I don't know why you..."

"Because there's something between us, and we both know it." He lifted his hand to her cheek and absorbed the gaze that fell upon him. "I know there's a reason for everything. There's a reason my grandmother chose this mortuary. There's a reason she showed herself to you and asked you to do what she's asked you to do. She put us in each other's path, and I'm grateful for that. I know we're really strangers. But every happy couple started out as strangers once, right?"

She didn't answer with words. Instead, she rose on her toes and wrapped her arms around his neck. She locked her eyes with his one more time before she pressed her warm lips to his.

"I feel it down deep inside of me that this is what's supposed to happen. You and me. Is that crazy?" she asked.

"Yes. It's crazy in the most wonderful way," he said as he placed a kiss on her forehead. "Let's go talk to her. I don't think I can take any more of the suspense."

Grace eased back and smile. "The room smells like roses. She's waiting for us."

BEFORE GRACE OPENED THE DOOR, she knew he could smell the roses. He taken a deep breath and then cleared his throat, though she imagined he was fighting off the tears.

"Mr. Kurtz is in his casket, and just to the right of the door."

The corner of his mouth turned up into a crooked smile. "You do that with all the families, don't you?"

"Do what?"

"Tell them how the room is laid out so that there are no surprises."

She acknowledged that with a nod. "Especially when it comes to families, people don't like to see their loved ones not living."

The other side of his mouth turned up and completed the smile. "They don't want to see them dead, is that what you're trying to say?"

"However, you want to take it. Yes, I walk into these rooms with other people in the same manner. In this case, you don't know Mr. Kurtz. But I don't want you to be startled or have a heart attack either."

Matthew reached out and touched her shoulder as she turned the knob on the door. "Has that happened? Have you had people have heart attacks?"

Grace let go of the doorknob. "Imagine if you are a mother, and your child was on the other side of that door. Or the woman you've been married to for sixty years was being laid to rest. Some people are comforted by knowing that their loved one looks peaceful. Others are only reminded this will be the last time they ever see them."

"You have had bad experiences here?"

"Of course. Passing is as unique to the person as it is to the family. It's equally as disturbing when you've prepared someone, and no one shows to visit."

Matthew scrubbed his hand over his face. "And here I am getting a second chance."

"I'll admit, it's an amazing gift. I don't appreciate it, but it's an amazing gift. You smelled the roses, didn't you?"

Matthew nodded now. "I suppose that's why I'm stalling in the hallway. I was with her when she died.

And I didn't get worked up when I saw her in the casket. But smelling the roses and knowing that I'll be able to talk to her again, I'm a little nervous."

"Remember, the room will be silent for you. Or, so I assume. After all, you are the one that heard her in the cemetery."

Matthew rubbed his hand over the back of his neck and swallowed hard. "Oh crap. You're right. I like to think I'm a strong man, but now I'm not sure."

Grace reached out and took his hand. She interlaced their fingers as they had on the drive. "We do this together."

"I have this feeling it won't be the only time."

Now it was her turn to smile at him. "Perhaps not. Your grandmother has some high expectations for me with this skill. I might need some help."

"Fulfilling last goodbyes?"

She reached for the doorknob. "Yes."

Matthew bent down and kissed her one more time softly on the lips. "I'm game." He took in one more breath and let it out slowly. "Open the door. I think I'm ready."

CHAPTER 23

*a*gain, Matthew was nearly dizzy with the scent of roses.

Mr. Kurtz, as promised, was to his right behind the door. The older gentleman, dressed in a gray suit, lay peacefully in his casket with his hands folded over his stomach.

Matthew stopped in the middle of the room and pressed his fingers to his temples. Seriously, if his grandmother was that close, did she have to make him dizzy?

"Do you want me to get you a chair?" Grace asked as she watched him.

"I thought the scent of the roses was making me dizzy, but I think I'm holding my breath."

She smiled, but she didn't laugh. "I'll pull over a couple of chairs anyway. Mr. Kurtz is curious as to what's going on."

Matthew turned as she pulled two chairs toward the center of the room. "He's talking to you now? You can hear him?"

"Yes." Grace sat down in the chair, and Matthew followed. She folded her hands neatly in her lap yet

153

leaned in toward casket. "His name is Matthew Campbell. He is Nora Campbell's grandson."

Matthew watched as Grace's face changed as though she could hear something he could not. "He's talking to you right now?"

She nodded with a hum. "He says he knows why we are here," she said as she looked toward Matthew. "He says that Nora is with him and wants to assure you that I'm not crazy."

He saw the pink fill her cheeks as she shifted her gaze to her hands.

"I don't think you're crazy."

"All the same, she wants me to ask you to ask her something that only she would know."

Suddenly Matthew's mind went blank. There were so many things he wanted to ask her, but how come he couldn't come up with this one thing.

"When I was little, when Grandma and I first started making our little newspaper, I was in charge of the weather page." He watched as Grace's eyes lifted and smiled into his. "I would always do a three-day forecast, but the yellow crayon was missing from her box of crayons. I never colored the sunshine yellow. What color was it?"

Grace sat for a moment and her eyes again shifted to her hands. He watched her nod as though she were taking in the information.

When she turned her head to look at him, he knew she had the right answer even before she said it. "The weather map in the Nora and Matthew newspaper was colored in periwinkle. News reporter Matthew Campbell also added temperatures to the forecast. And, because he thought bigger was better, temperatures always ranged in the one hundreds."

Matthew felt the air whoosh from his lungs as he

leaned forward placing his elbows on his knees, and his head in his hands.

She had more detail than periwinkle. The only other person that could have told Grace about the temperatures or the color of his sun was his mother and his grandfather. He knew for a fact his mother hadn't spoken to Grace.

"You are talking to her," he said as he lifted his head. "Oh my God, you can talk to my grandmother."

Grace reached for his hand and gave it a squeeze. "Yes, I can. She has a million things to say, and I'm not very sure Mr. Kurtz is happy about it." She laughed as she pressed a kiss to Matthew's fingers. "He can hardly keep up with everything she's telling him."

"What is she saying?"

"That she's happy you're not with Rebecca Barnes."

Matthew chuckled. "Honestly, that was never going to be a problem," he said to the air above Mr. Kurtz's casket, as if that might be where his grandmother loomed.

"She wants you to take a rosebush to your mother's house and put one in your backyard too." Grace shook her head and looked at him. "She would like me to have a rosebush too."

"This weekend. We'll plant it this weekend." This time he gave her hand a squeeze. "What else is she telling you?"

Grace sat still for a moment. "She wants you to help me pass on final goodbyes. She says every person that passes through here has something to say. You're well-connected, and I'm connected to her."

"People will get suspicious, won't they?"

"That's what I think," Grace admitted, and then held her hands up in surrender. "That set her off."

"Now you're in trouble." He let out a laugh. "When Grandma Nora gets mad, nobody's happy."

Grace pursed her lips. "She wants me to smack you in the back of the head."

He felt the blood drain from his cheeks. "Yeah, you're talking to her."

"She says the story you're planning to do on Mr. Leeds and Mr. Rodriguez is very honorable. She's proud of you."

Matthew batted away the tears that were forming in his eyes. "I miss her."

"She says she knows. But she'll always be right here." He watched as Grace brushed away a tear that rolled down her cheek. "She says she's glad we found each other. She says we are destined."

Matthew lifted his hand to Grace's cheek and wiped away another tear. "I think I knew that from the first moment I met you. This isn't an easy circumstance to build a new relationship on."

"That part is up to us, she says. And she hopes were as happy as she was."

Matthew looked around the room. "Scent of roses is gone."

Grace nodded. "Mr. Kurtz said she's gone."

"Gone? What does that mean? That's all she had? Is she going to come back?"

"Let's just say she left the conversation. She did what she needed to do. She told you she was here."

"She freaking turned on all the lights," he reminded her.

And at that moment, the lights turned off in the room.

He heard Grace laugh as he heard her stand up and move toward the wall. A moment later the lights came back on at Grace's hand. "Your grandmother has a sense of humor."

"If that's what you call it."

"She's given me a mission, and I think I'm ready to accept it. I don't know that I can process a final goodbye to every person passes through here, but I'll do my best."

Matthew stood and moved to her. Gathering her hands in his, he lifted her fingers to his lips and kissed each one. "I'll be right here with you if you'll have me."

"I'm scared of this, of us."

"I'm not," he admitted. "When you know something is right, you just know. In another week, we will have known each other longer. Every day we're going to learn something new. All I know is that I want to be with you. Not just for a moment or for a year, but forever."

"I guess we'll figure this all out."

"Why don't we go to your place, just for a drink or something. I need to calm my nerves."

Grace bit down on her bottom lip. "I have never trusted a man enough to bring him back to my house."

Matthew stepped back and gave her a quizzical look. "Never?"

"Never. Perhaps that's why my relationships never worked. My home, my sanctuary."

"You're telling me we're not going back to your place?"

Grace stepped toward him and wrapped her arms around his neck and in turn, he placed his hands on her hips and pulled her in close. "Actually, I'm telling you I trust you enough to be the first man in my home."

"That's quite a responsibility."

"Seems like we're taking on a lot of that." Grace turned back toward the casket. "Mr. Kurtz kindly suggests that we leave him be. He is tired, and anxious for his funeral."

Matthew pressed his forehead to hers. "Tell him thank you for being the vessel that delivered the messages to us."

"I will. Go ahead," she said as she stepped back from him. "Let me get Mr. Kurtz settled, and I'll meet you at the front."

Grace brushed a kiss across his lips and then opened the door for him to leave.

As he walked out into the hallway, which was still well lit, he tried to absorb everything that had just happened. Grace had told him things nobody else knew. There was no doubt in his mind that his grandmother had been in the room. And to top it all off, he knew he had fallen in love with Grace.

No one had ever twisted him up like she did or made him want to think about forever. It was crazy to think he loved someone he'd only known for a week. Even crazier to think that that same woman could talk to his grandmother. And again, he reminded himself that his grandmother was dead.

But when he thought about the week he had had, it intrigued him. Just over a week ago he watched as his grandmother passed away—he held her hand as she slipped to the other side. He consoled his parents, his sibling, and his aunts. He cried in the shower were no one else could see him. And he winced when he thought about sleeping in the same bed with Rebecca Barnes.

God, what a week.

And in that week he had met Grace. Grace, with her soothing touch and voice. The woman who did everything to comfort everyone. In that week she divulged her deepest secret to him.

What he felt for Grace went further than this common bond around his grandmother. Yes, he was smart enough to understand he was grieving and shouldn't make big decisions. Yes, he should give it more time before he decided that he was head over heels in love with someone. But this was Grace.

There was just something about the woman that made him want to be with her all the time.

Maybe he should just kiss her goodbye and go home. He'd see her again tomorrow. And on the weekend, because they were going to talk to the gentleman over the ballgame.

Then again, maybe he should just be a man and tell her how he felt. Of course, the very thought made him chuckle, what man ever told anyone how they felt?

Matthew rubbed his eyes. What he would do was go to Grace's house, have a glass of wine, and kiss her goodnight. He would leave like a true gentleman, no matter how bad he wanted to stay, and then tomorrow he would talk to his mother. Aside from his grandmother, she was the wisest woman he'd ever known.

He had fallen in love with the girl at the mortuary. What was his mother going to say to that?

CHAPTER 24

*G*race humored herself as she drove home, thinking about the fact there was a man in a car following her. She was glad to have the drive time alone. It gave her time to process what she'd done. She'd invited a man to her house.

What she had to remember was this was no ordinary man. Never in her thirty-three years had she had a man in her home. And when she'd told him that, she'd meant it.

Oh, she was no prude, but she'd had other priorities in her life. Before she got her own place, her roommate had plenty of men over, and that never turned out well. Grace found that occupying herself with her work was a better fit. If she'd spent the night with a man, it was usually at his place. Perhaps she just hadn't wanted to live where her judgment could be skewed.

Maybe she was just waiting for the perfect man to invite into her home. And just as she had that thought, she could smell the roses, and then they faded away again.

Was there anyone else in the world that was part of a matchmaking scheme compliments of a spirit?

As she turned down her street, and Matthew followed, she caught herself smiling in the mirror.

She'd never felt about another man the way she felt about Matthew, even if she'd only known him a week. It felt much longer. They felt connected.

Of course, she couldn't help but wonder if he felt that too. The way he gazed into her eyes, and the feelings that stirred in her when he kissed her—certainly he felt it.

Grace pulled into her driveway and opened the garage door with the button on her visor. As she parked inside, Matthew pulled his car behind hers and climbed out after shutting off the engine.

"Is it okay for me to park here?"

"Of course. I'm not going anywhere if you're here with me," she said as she pulled her bag out of the backseat.

"I wasn't sure if you had a roommate."

For the first time, she considered that maybe she should have told him that. After all, there were easing into this relationship. What would it hurt to have him wonder if someone else might walk through the door? It would keep him on the up and up, right?

Then she thought of the rose scent that had filled her car. Why would Nora Campbell have put her in harm's way?

"I should have offered to stop and get a bottle of wine or something," Matthew said still standing just beyond the threshold of the garage door.

"It just so happens that I have a new bottle of wine inside, and enough food in the refrigerator that we surely can come up with something if we get hungry.

"Girl Scout?"

"Just a wannabe. But I'm usually prepared for anything. Boy Scout?"

He laughed. "Yes, and I suck at preparedness."

And there she'd learned just a little more about the man.

He took her bag, the one she always toted in from the house to the car and to work. Grace unlocked the door and pushed it in. Then, she walked into her house, and Matthew followed.

IT WAS FEMININE. Those were his first thoughts upon entering Grace's house. Honestly, he'd have expected nothing less.

The house itself didn't look to be more than a thousand square feet, but it had to be a hundred years old.

"The kitchen is in the back. You can drop the bag in the living room," Grace said as she continued in.

Matthew turned to drop the bag, and he smiled at the small, overstuffed couch with soft pillows and a pink throw over the back of it. There was one more chair in the room, and the desk Grace had told him about. There wasn't even a television in the living room.

As he was told, he dropped the bag and followed her to the kitchen, which was thoroughly modern.

"Did you flip this house?"

She smiled at him. "I painted the walls. My brother did the hardwood, and he and his friend tried their hand at the kitchen. They did pretty well, but we did have a professional come in and tweak a few things they just couldn't get right. They were trying to get the hang of flipping a house, but I think they got bored."

"How old is this house?" he asked as he looked at the ornate trim around the doors and the floor.

"It was built in 1896."

"Nothing in this town is that old," he said as he watched her pull wine glasses from the cupboard.

"The six houses on this street are." Grace opened a drawer and took out a wine opener. "The building where we turned was the original grocery store for the area. After the grocery store moved because it needed more space, they turned it into a post office."

"And now it's a craft brewery?"

"Yes."

Grace opened the small blade on the wine opener, and Matthew moved in. "Let me do that," he offered, taking the opener and the bottle of wine.

Perhaps it was the child in him, but he always loved cutting the wax from the top of a bottle and pulling out the cork, just to hear the pop.

When he'd been fully satisfied with the procedure, he turned and poured them each a generous glass.

He handed Grace a glass and kept one for himself. "Here's to new beginnings."

"New beginnings," she repeated as she tapped her glass to his and then drank. A moment later she winced and shook her head.

"It's not good?" he asked taking a sip and then another.

"It's fine. I'm not a wine drinker. I want to be, but seriously, it just isn't my taste."

"Then why do you have a bottle?"

Grace laughed and opened her cabinet. Stacked inside were bottles of every shade. "This is how people say thank you for making my grandmother look at peace. I get baskets full of wine, fruit, cookies, you name it. I just don't happen to drink wine."

"Thank goodness I sent you flowers."

"From your family," she said, and Matthew shook his head.

"From me. I wanted you to know I was thinking of you."

Grace set her glass down on the counter and moved to him swiftly, wrapping her arms around his neck. Her lips came to his, soft, and open.

Struggling to balance himself against the counter, Matthew set his glass down and entangled his fingers into Grace's hair as she pressed her body against him.

He'd hoped they'd get to this during the evening, it had been on his mind all day. And, he figured she must have gotten over the anxiety of having a man in her house.

Grace's hands pressed against his chest. No doubt she could feel his heart hammering away. If she pressed any closer to him, that wasn't all she was going to feel. God, it had been a long time since a woman worked him up like this.

A moment later Grace broke the kiss and stepped back. He expected her to look regretful, and he'd give her that, it was unnecessary, but he was learning she was a bit of a prim and proper type. Getting a man worked up in her home was not her style.

Had he made any bets on what was to happen next, he would have lost.

Grace gripped the front of his shirt and began to drag him through the kitchen and into the living room, where she let go of her grip on his clothing and took his hand.

She led him to that overstuffed couch and proceeded to throw off all the cute pillows she had to have taken so much time arranging. Then, she lowered herself to the couch and pulled him down on her.

"Are you sure you want to be doing this?" Matthew asked between gasps of air. "I can go home. I don't want to pressure you into..."

BERNADETTE MARIE

Her mouth came back to his and silenced him.

"I really don't want to think about anything else right this moment. I have it under good authority that you're a decent man, and you're here for the long haul."

Shouldn't that have been his turn off? He knew where she got that information, but he couldn't stop himself now as Grace's fingers worked against the buttons on his shirt, and then her palms were pressed to his bare skin.

It was a lost cause now. Those feelings he'd been having, the ones he'd wanted to talk to his mother about, they were bursting in his chest now.

Before they could go any further, he pushed himself up and looked down at Grace. Her eyes gazed up at him, and his heart ached at the sexy pout on her lips.

"I want to tell you something," he said as she pulled her hands back from his skin and balled them into fists.

"Don't you dare tell me you really are in love with Rebecca Barnes."

The sheer horror of the statement made him chuckle, and he nipped her lips with a kiss before perching above her again.

"No. No. God no."

Her eyes softened, and so did her hands.

"What?"

"I've been thinking about this all day, and though it doesn't seem like the right time, it most defiantly seems like the right time."

Grace cupped his face in her hands. "What are you trying to say?"

"I've never, ever, felt this way about anyone before."

"What way? You've done this before, right?" Again,

panic filled her eyes. "I mean, are you the only thirty-something man out there that hasn't done this?"

"What? No." He shook his head and laughed. "I've done this. And I'm thirty-five, by the way. And never with Rebecca to clear that up right now, and again."

Grace laughed, and even the quake of her body in laughter set his blood racing through his veins.

"What are you trying to say?" Her voice dripped of suggestion, even as she laughed.

"I've never loved anyone."

Grace's eyes went wide, and the laughter stopped. "Oh."

"Yeah. I've thought that I wanted to tell you, but it was too early. Much too early, right? I mean, we've known each other a week. But I can't help it. I can't…"

"Is this the reporter in you?"

"What?"

"The incessant talking."

"I'm not…" he took a breath and realized he was rambling.

Grace wrapped her arms around him again, now her fingers gripped his hair, and she pulled him back to her mouth. "I've never had a man tell me he loved me before."

"I made a mess of it."

She shook her head, her nose shimming across his. "Oh, no you didn't. It was very romantic."

"Then my idea of romance is messed up."

"Matthew," her voice was soft and filled with heat. "I feel the same way."

He let out a little breath. "You do?"

"Yes. It's crazy, but I love you too."

"And what do we do with that? What's next?"

"Let's finish what we've started here, and then we can make plans."

Again, their mouths joined, and the heat between them intensified as he brushed his fingers under her blouse on her soft, delicate skin.

Matthew eased back up again. "I swear if I smell roses during this, it will scar me for life."

Grace let out a loud laugh. "I have no doubt she's going to leave us alone. Now, stop talking."

CHAPTER 25

*H*e'd stopped talking. In fact, Matthew wasn't sure he'd uttered another coherent phrase the rest of the night.

When sunlight filled the room, she was there with him, wrapped in his arms. Grace's hair splayed over his arm, and her breath was warm on his chest. God, he never wanted to move again. If he were going to die, this would be as good a time as any.

As he breathed in the scent of her, he swore he could smell the faint fragrance of roses.

"There is a breeze, and the window is open," Grace said, her voice still full of sleep. "The bush out back is in full bloom, and you can smell it. Don't panic," she whispered against his skin.

Matthew kissed the top of her head.

"How did you know what I was thinking?"

"Soulmate, remember? You called me that last night."

He squeezed his eyes tightly and thought about it. Yes, he had. They were in the bathtub, buried to their necks in bubbles, and he told her he thought they were soulmates. What he remembered most was that she didn't laugh. Instead, she had sighed, as if the words had pleased her.

His stomach rumbled. "Tell me you have something for breakfast that would satisfy that."

Grace rolled back, the sheet that had covered her shifted, and she didn't tug it back up to cover herself. Comfort, he thought. They were absolutely comfortable together.

"I have cereal, but I don't know if the milk is any good. I might have a granola bar." She ran her fingers through her hair and then lazily stretched. "I could grab a shower, and we could go get some breakfast."

Matthew gathered her back up in his arms. "I have to get home and get ready to head out on location."

"Fireworks on the river." She nuzzled her face against his chest. "This is the first year I'd rather not go. I want to stay right here."

Matthew ran his hand down her hair. "Let's meet back here after then. Or you could stay at my house."

Grace pulled back and looked at him through sleepy eyes. "Let's sleep in your bed. I want to see what your place looks like."

"It's nothing special."

"Oh, it'll tell me everything I need to know."

He kissed the top of her head. "It's a date." Stroking a finger down her throat, he gazed into her sleepy eyes. "I have to go. What time will you and your family get down to the river?"

"We usually get there around noon. Dad likes to set up the corn-hole and challenge my brother."

"I'll find you." He kissed her lightly on the lips. "What are they going to think of this?"

Grace looked down at her naked, exposed body. "I didn't have any plans to tell them about this. I share a lot with them, but I wasn't going to tell them everything."

Now he laughed. "Okay, what are they going to think about us?"

She pressed her cheek against his chest again. "I don't think it's going to take them by surprise."

MATTHEW WASN'T sure if the sun was brighter, or if it was just his mood. He'd spent the night in the arms of the woman he loved, whom he'd only known for a week, but it was right. God, it was just right.

His head filled with all the things that were to come. How long should they date? He already knew he wanted to marry her. What more could she do with the power she had to talk to the dead?

That thought caught him off guard.

Was that psychological? Was he worried about that? Did it bother him? Was he hoping it would help him in some way?

At a stoplight, Matthew rubbed his temples and took a breath. Her gift of talking to those that already passed had nothing to do with him. In fact, had he not been there when the lights turned on in the mortuary or heard her tell him things that only his grandmother would know, he wasn't sure he would have believed her, and wouldn't that have been a shame. At that moment, with the lust induced fog in his head, he couldn't even imagine a moment without Grace in it anymore.

Matthew pulled up in front of his townhome and parked his car on the street. He gathered his items out of the passenger seat and closed the door when he heard the voice.

"Good morning, Matthew," Rebecca said from his front step.

He hadn't even seen her sitting there.

Inside he felt his stomach churn. Seriously, this wasn't what he needed right now.

"Good morning, Rebecca."

She'd been crying, he could see it even behind her dark sunglasses. Her nose and cheeks were red, and her lip looked as though she'd been chewing on it for hours.

"Is something wrong?" He had to ask. She was his friend after all.

"I've been here all night. I was waiting for you."

"Why?"

"Why?" Her voice grew in pitch and volume. "You need me."

No, no he didn't. Of course, now, sitting on his step crying, he knew she was crazy. This must have been what his grandmother was so upset about.

"Rebecca, I'm fine."

"You're in mourning."

Matthew nodded. "I am. I miss my grandmother terribly, but I'm going to be okay. You don't have to keep checking in on me."

"I don't think you understand. I'm here for you. You need companionship, but you keep pushing me away."

It was then that Matthew noticed there were others on the street. The last thing he needed was to be recognized while arguing with a woman on his front step.

"Let's go inside and talk. I don't have much time. I have to be on location soon."

Rebecca pulled her sunglasses off and scanned a critical look over him. "Where have you been? Those are the clothes you had on yesterday."

He hadn't seen her yesterday, so that didn't sit well with him.

"Let's go in and talk."

She bit down on her lip again and nodded as she rose.

Matthew slipped past her and unlocked the door, then held it for her as she passed.

"Can I get you some coffee?" he asked continuing to the kitchen, where he laid the items in his hands on the counter. "I have that blend you like from Hawaii."

"Yes, I would like that," she said, and her voice was softer now.

She sat down at the breakfast bar as he started the coffee.

Matthew, who was a professional at leading a conversation was at a loss for words. He thought he should call the station and let them know he'd be meeting the crew at the river. Something told him he wasn't going to get Rebecca out of his house quickly.

"So, what have…"

"You never answered me. Where were you last night," she interrupted as Matthew scooped coffee grounds into the filter.

He stood with his back to her for another moment before turning around.

"I was out, but I don't see where that's your business."

Her cheeks were fiery red, and her eyes mad with anger. "You were out? With who? You're not the kind of man who stays out all night at bars or things like that. If you were out all night, and coming home with sleep-tousled hair, in the same clothes you wore yesterday, then you were with someone."

Now the anger building up in him set fire. "I didn't see you yesterday. How do you know I have on the same clothes I had on yesterday?"

"I saw you."

"You saw me? Where? Because you sure as hell didn't let me know you saw me."

"I see you all the time. I know you've been spending a lot of time at the cemetery and the mortuary. Do you have some newly dead friends there?" The bite in her voice had him fisting his hands to his side.

"It's none of your business why I was there."

"I know you're spending time with that woman from the mortuary. The one that spends all of her time with dead people. Don't you think that's rather odd?"

Matthew flattened his hands on the counter and stared at the woman sitting there. What had happened to Rebecca? She wasn't some psycho, she was simply a little pushy, but this was going too far.

"It's her job to make people presentable after they passed, and she does one hell of a job."

"And you liked her work so much you thought you'd sleep with her?"

"Yes." The word flew from his mouth, and it felt vile. That wasn't why he'd slept with Grace. He'd slept with Grace because he'd fallen in love with her. "Grace and I have something very special."

"Grace? Her name is Grace?" The tears poured from Rebecca's eyes now, and his instinct was to go to her and hold her, but not now. Not today.

"Yes, her name is Grace, and she's a spectacular woman. I'm in love with her."

He watched as the sobbing blonde in front of him switched from sadness to anger as she hopped off the stool and moved toward him. "You're in love with her?" Her words were spat with a venom Matthew sore he could feel in his chest.

"Yes. I'm in love with Grace. I spent the night with

her yesterday, and I'm spending the day with her and her family today."

"You always spend the day with your family at the river."

"And they will be there too."

She moved toward him, and he backed up until he hit the counter.

"I slept in your bed not even a week ago, and now you tell me you love someone else?"

He held up his hands and pressed them to her shoulders as she inched even closer. "You slept in my bed as a friend. We didn't make love, and I never promised you anything."

His words seemed to strike her as hard as his fists might have.

Rebecca stumbled back clutching her chest. "You don't want me," she sobbed.

"We are only friends. I thought you understood that."

"But...but..." she stuttered her words as she continued to back away from him. "I thought we had a chance."

"Rebecca, I've never felt that way about you."

She steadied herself with her hands on the back of one of the stools at the bar and took in a few intentional breaths.

"You don't love me."

"No. I never have."

"So, all of this was..."

"I don't know," he admitted. "It was a friendship from a long time ago that just always resurfaced. I wasn't looking for love when I found it. But I found it with Grace."

She nodded as she batted her eyes, which were full of tears. "Right. Grace."

Rebecca stood straight and placed her dark sunglasses back on her face.

"I hope you and this Grace will be very happy. I'm done, Matthew. You won't see me ever again."

"Rebecca…" He reached for her, and she stepped back.

"I would have married you and made you very happy. You'll regret this, Matthew Campbell. I promise you. You'll regret this."

He watched as she stormed out of his kitchen, and then the front door slammed closed.

Matthew leaned up against the kitchen counter and pressed his fingers to his eyes. It shouldn't bother him, the way that Rebecca felt. He didn't love her. He never told her he loved her, and he never promised her anything. Grace—that was a different story. He did love her. He did make love to her. And he'd promise her the moon if he thought she wanted it.

Rebecca was confused. That was all. In time, she'd remarry again, and it would just be water under the bridge.

So why was he worked up inside over it?

When his cell phone rang, his mind snapped back to the moment. It was his cameraman.

"Hey, man. I'm going to have to meet you guys at the river. Something came up, and I'm running behind."

When he disconnected the call, he thought of calling Grace. At that very moment, he needed her.

Instead, he texted her. *I love you.*

As soon as the text sent, he smelled the roses. "Thanks for the help, Grandma. Maybe you can make her stay away from me," he said on a laugh as he finished the coffee and headed up to his room to get ready for the picnic at the river.

CHAPTER 26

*G*race was happy Matthew had left when he had. She'd had just enough time to shower and get ready before her mother showed up on her doorstep.

That had been the plan all along, but when she started kissing Matthew the night before, nothing else in the world mattered to her.

He'd told her he loved her. Just thinking about it made her feel as though she were floating on air.

Grace picked up her phone from the counter when it chimed and read the text. She felt the heat move right to her cheeks as she returned the text. *I love you too.*

"Who just texted you? You're grinning like a kid on Christmas," her mother said as she stirred the potato salad they had just made.

"Don't worry about it."

"I'm your mother. I'm going to worry about it. Was it a man?"

Grace slid her phone into her pocket and went back to her task of making sandwiches. Her mother, however, set down the spoon, crossed her arms, and watched her.

"You're going to flat out lie to your mother?"

"I'm not lying. I said don't worry about it."

"If my daughter is seeing someone, I want to know. I'm going to have to meet him, and I want to make sure I'm not taken by surprise."

"You won't be. You already know him," Grace admitted as she slathered mayonnaise on bread.

Her mother picked back up the spoon and stirred thoughtfully. "I already know him," she hummed to herself. "Not...no. Maybe...nah."

Grace laughed at her mother whispering the conversation to the salad as she mixed, and then her head popped up, and her eyes grew wide. "Oh, you're not really dating Nora Campbell's grandson, are you?"

Grace was surprised at her mother's lack of delight. "You don't sound enthused."

"Grace, he's one of the family members. He's in mourning. Seriously, how did you let that happen?"

Well, she thought her mother would have been more supportive. In fact, she was quite disappointed that she had anything to say on the matter.

"I understand. And we've talked about that."

"You've talked about it? It hasn't even been a week since her funeral. Grace..."

"Mom, I'm thirty-years-old. I can handle this. He's adjusting just fine. It was his grandmother after all, and she was expected to pass. It's not like she got killed in a car accident and was young and doing something foolish."

Her mother's lips tightened. "You're going to get hurt by this."

"I am not. Besides his grandmother orchestrated the whole thing."

Her mother put down the spoon again and turned

her back on her while she fidgeted with something on the table.

"Now you have nothing to say?" Grace scolded and then wished she hadn't.

"You've been talking to Nora Campbell? Grace, I thought you took great steps to not do that."

"I do, usually." She wiped off her hands and went to her mother. "I went in without my headphones, and she caught me. She was very adamant about Matthew and me, and well, it worked. Mom, I think I love him."

Her mother's lips twitched between a smile and a frown but settled on the frown. "Grace, this is crazy. You can't know you love someone…"

"I know I love him, Mom. Please give me this. I've hidden away with my work for so long because someone was going to come along and think I'm crazy, but he doesn't."

"And he knows you talk to his grandmother?"

"Yes."

With a huff, her mother turned back to the potato salad and began to cover it with plastic wrap.

"I think you're crazy, Grace. Your brother is going to…"

"Have to deal with it. Mom, this isn't for anyone else to decide. This is my life. This is my gift or curse, depending on how you look at it. It's mine to share with whomever I want to know." She touched her mother's shoulder. "I know what I'm doing. I'm going to be fine, and when you get to know him, you're going to love him."

Her mother finished with the salad and stood still for a moment. "They were a very gracious and kind family."

"They are."

"I'm sure he's a nice boy."

"He's a man, Mom. He has a good career, a kind heart, and he loves me. I know it's fast and I know I just met him, but I know what I feel."

And just as she'd expected in the first place, her mother softened and pulled her in for a hug. "I'll always worry about you. You know that."

"I wouldn't expect anything else."

"When do I officially get to meet him, and not as a family member that passed through the doors, but as the man my daughter loves?"

Grace gave her mother a squeeze. "He will be at the river. He's doing a remote broadcast, and he's going to join us."

"That's right. He's the TV guy."

"Reporter."

Her mother nodded. "I look forward to seeing him."

* * *

THE SUN WAS high in the sky, and Matthew was melting in his Polo shirt with the news station logo on it.

Days at the river for all of the festivities were one of his favorite memories, but working the crowd and standing in the sun, it was killing him. He'd rather be under one of the umbrellas or tents with a cold drink in his hand enjoying a conversation with Grace.

"Matthew, we have three minutes until we go live for a cut-in," Kyle adjusted the tripod in front of Matthew.

"I'm ready."

When he looked up from his marker, he saw Grace standing just beyond Kyle, her mother at her side. His heart raced when she lifted her hand in a wave.

"I'll be right back," he told Kyle as he passed him and went to Grace.

He wanted to scoop her up and give her a kiss, but he refrained. Instead, he held out his hand to her mother.

"Mrs. Carter, it's nice to see you again."

The smile that formed on her lips was genuine, and he was grateful for that.

"Hello, Mr. Campbell."

"Please, call me Matthew."

She took the hand he offered. "And you can call me Martha."

Grace stepped in and hugged him, then stayed close enough to keep an arm around him. "Are you getting ready to go live?"

"Yeah. I have a cut-in in just a minute, then a three-minute segment for the news at noon. I'll have a few more cut-ins throughout the day for the five, six, and ten o'clock spots."

Martha laughed. "They do keep you busy, don't they."?

"They do. I'd rather report about firework displays than traffic accidents."

"I don't blame you a bit. Do you have family here today?"

"My family comes a little later," he told her.

"We are set up over just beyond the bandstand. You can't miss our tents. Please have your family join us when they get here."

The nerves in his stomach settled. "I will do that."

"I'll let you two chat," she offered. "Good luck on your cut-in."

He turned to see Kyle waving him back.

Matthew turned to Grace. "I have to go. You can stay and watch if you want. I'll be about five more minutes."

"I'll wait," she said before she kissed him on the cheek. "Sorry. I shouldn't do that when you're in public."

With that, he took her face in his hands and pressed a long kiss on her lips. "We're not going to worry about it."

When he walked back to his marker, Kyle shook his head. "Seriously, man. We don't have time for kissing women."

"There is always time to kiss women," he said as he adjusted his earpiece and heard Pamela, the anchor, chuckle about what he'd said. A moment later they were back from commercial break, and Kyle was counting down.

But just beyond the camera stood the woman he loved. Though he missed his grandmother, and the grief was horrendous, seeing Grace standing there smiling at him filled his every need.

*a*n overabundance of food, sun, and a few sangrias that her father made had Grace leaning back in her lawn chair considering a short nap before the dancing began and the fireworks lit the sky.

Her mother had warmed up to Matthew just fine, and luckily so did her brother and father. She wasn't sure how many rounds of corn hole they had conned him to play, but he was getting quite good at it.

He'd gone off to do his five o'clock cut-in, and then his segment, which he was going to head over to the pie eating contest for that.

Grace had chosen to sit back and absorb the noise and the conversations around her.

Matthew's mother and father had joined them with their picnic. She enjoyed hearing his mother go on and on about how her family had eased them through Nora's death.

They continued with stories of the woman that Nora had been, and there was nothing but praise for her. And, since Grace could faintly smell roses, she knew Nora was enjoying the conversation as well.

Grace lifted the last of her sangria to her lips as

she watched Matthew walking toward her. He was frantically texting. Something had happened between the moment he knocked her brother out of their corn hole championship and his news segment.

Easing up in her chair she watched him walk toward her.

"Everything okay?" she asked as she pushed herself to her feet and swayed briefly before gaining her balance.

"What? Yeah," he said looking up from his phone and then back down at it. He finished a text and shoved his phone back in his pocket. A smile replaced the frown on his lips. "You want to go for a walk down the river? I have an hour before I need to do another segment."

Grace nodded and reached out her hand for him to take. She knew there were plenty of eyes on them, there was no need to tell anyone where they were going.

Hundreds of people lined the river walk. Children ran and laughed. Adults ate picnics and stood in groups talking. Blankets and umbrellas littered the lawn as others lay with their eyes closed absorbing the sights and sounds, just as Grace had been doing.

There were the few that called out to Matthew, recognizing him from TV. He kindly would wave and give them a smile, all the while holding tightly to Grace's hand. But he didn't say a word as they walked.

They had walked to the furthest point of the path to where it would turn and go under the bridge and into downtown, and he still hadn't said a word.

Grace slowed her walk, forcing him to do the same. She gave him a gentle tug and stopped walking.

"Something happened, and you're going to have to walk all the way around the city before you let go of it at this rate. What happened?" she finally asked in the shade of a small oak grove which the path forked around.

Matthew stood looking down at her and gathered her other hand in his. "You can read me just fine, can't you?"

"You told me you loved me. And I told you the same. I don't think we would have done that if we weren't connected enough to know when one of us was hurting."

He gave her hands a squeeze. "I'm not hurting. Maybe a little confused. Let's sit for a moment."

He led her to a park bench among the oaks and dropped his arm around her shoulder when he sat next to her.

"Okay, Mr. Campbell, spill it. What's going on?"

Matthew pulled his phone from his pocket and scrolled back through the text messages.

"When I got home this morning, Rebecca was sitting on my doorstep. She'd been there all night."

Grace worked hard to not let the disappointment show on her face. "What did she want?"

"Me."

"Oh," she sighed, and her voice betrayed her by shaking.

"Don't panic. I didn't do anything with Rebecca." He moved his arm from around her shoulders and leaned both of his elbows on his knees as he scrolled through the long line of text messages. "I guess my grandmother had reason to worry. Rebecca seemed to think there was a lot more going on between us than I did. I made a huge mistake letting her stay with me the other night. She read a lot into that."

"That's understandable." After all, Grace let him stay the night, and it came with a whole lot of expectations.

"No, it's understandable that you and I expect something out of our situation," he said as if he knew what she was thinking. "But it wasn't like that with Rebecca." He buried his face in his hands. "God, I led her on. I kissed her, Grace." Quickly he sat straight and looked her in the eye. "Not this morning, but before my grandmother's funeral."

Grace let go of the breath that lodged itself in her lungs.

"Okay. What else?"

"We kissed, and she slept with me—slept. We've made that clear, right?"

Grace nodded. "But she thinks it meant more?"

"Yes."

"You were distraught. This happens," she said feeling the twisting pain of her words. "Grief causes people to make choices they wouldn't make otherwise." The words she was trained to use burned her ears. The fear that she'd done exactly that, used his pain to get what she wanted, made her stomach churn.

"You think I did the same thing with you," he offered as he turned to look at her. "Don't you dare think that. Grace, what you and I have is real. My grandmother would have put a stop to it if it wasn't."

Grace eased back, realizing how stiff she'd become. "What happened with Rebecca?"

"She knew I hadn't been home. I think she must have been stalking me because she knew I still had on the same clothes I'd worn the day before. But I hadn't seen her. I was honest. I told her I'd stayed with someone, and she knew who. She knew it was you."

Grace leaned back against the bench and Matthew turned to face her.

"She got very worked up. She did some yelling and came at me, but nothing happened. She didn't hurt me or try to. Honestly, I think there's a layer to Rebecca that I just don't know. The decent person in me worries about her, and I shouldn't."

"Ah, but that's the problem like you said." She leaned to rest her head on his shoulder. "You're a decent person."

He handed Grace his phone, and she sat forward when she realized he was entrusting her with his problem. "She's been texting all day. One minute she's mad as hell at me for leading her on. The next she's apologetic and sad."

Grace scrolled through the text messages, and her chest ached as she read them. "I really think you should worry about her. I mean, I think she could be dangerous to you and to her."

"That's what's coming across." He took the phone back when she handed it to him. "I don't want something bad to happen to her, but at the same time, I never wanted anything with Rebecca. Yeah, okay, the company was nice when I was feeling down last week. I didn't know this is where I'd be," he said looking up into her eyes. "I didn't know I'd find you, that it would be more. And, Grace, it's so much more."

"Grace Carter?" The voice pulled Grace from the intimate conversation with Matthew to see a woman standing in front of her, and two more women behind her. "I'm sorry to interrupt. But you are Grace Carter, right?"

"Yes," she said slowly and then recognized the woman. "Mrs. Fallon, how are you?"

"I'm doing very well, my dear." She clasped her hands together. "I just knew that was you. I'd never forget such a kind face."

Grace smiled and stood up to be face to face with the woman. Matthew followed.

"Matthew, this is Mrs. Fallon."

He held out his hand to her. "It's a pleasure to meet you."

Mrs. Fallon's cheeks grew pink. "You're from TV, aren't you?"

"Yes, ma'am."

"I thought so. My husband loved to watch the news, and I got into the habit myself. He's been gone, oh, going on five years now."

"I'm sorry for your loss," Matthew offered.

"Grace and her family took care of us during that difficult time. He died too young from cancer."

"She recently helped my family as well. When my grandmother passed."

Mrs. Fallon let out a sigh of compassion before turning back to Grace. "Do you remember when you spoke to me about the support group for spouses left by cancer?"

"I do," Grace said. "Was that able to help you?"

"Not only did it help me, but I started my own group. I found there was a vast community of sixty-somethings that needed one another." Mrs. Fallon opened her purse and pulled out a card. "Here, per-haps you can share this with anyone you think might need us. We're more laid back than other support groups. In fact, we've even had a few members con-nect and get married."

"That is wonderful. I will keep this handy. So many people need this kind of support."

Mrs. Fallon smiled wide as she patted Grace's hand. "You are a gentle and kind soul." She shifted her eyes to Matthew. "Take care of this one. She's a keeper."

Matthew looked down at Grace. "I think she is too."

They said their goodbyes and Mrs. Fallon went

on her way, but the joy she'd brought to Grace in those few moments continued to resonate through her.

"Why don't we head back. I hear music."

"Dance floor must be open."

"Do you know how to swing dance?" Matthew asked.

Grace laughed. "I fall over my own feet. Dancing is not in my wheelhouse."

He took her hand and began to pull her back toward the crowd. "Let me be your teacher. I'll show you what the one and only Nora Campbell taught me, and I'll guarantee that by the end of the night we will be a crowd pleaser."

Grace wasn't sure about that, but she couldn't help but let him pull her back toward the music and onto the dance floor, all the while thinking that this was the kind of joy she wanted for the rest of her life.

CHAPTER 28

*N*othing could have pulled Grace's head from the clouds when she walked into the mortuary on Thursday morning.

She was exhausted, perhaps a little hungover, sunburned, and on an emotional high that nearly lifted her off her feet.

Matthew had spun her around the dance floor for hours. He'd been right. Whatever Nora had taught him, he was able to transfer to Grace, and she danced. She stood off to the side as he did his remote segments for the news, and then, wrapped in his arms and surrounded by her family, she watched the sky explode into beautiful colors to celebrate the country's independence.

Afterward, she slept in Matthew's arms in his bed, and she decided that she never wanted to spend another night alone.

"You look happy," her brother Scott stood at the front counter with Ella going over the day's schedule.

"I am happy, thank you. I had a very nice day yesterday. And, now I'm going to go get Mr. Kurtz ready for his funeral."

"His daughter already called four times to make sure the limos were going to be on time."

"The funeral isn't until ten-thirty. When did she start calling?"

"At seven."

Grace laughed. "Some people just want the best for their family."

"The chapel is set up. I think there is one arrangement that mom just received, and that's it. The printer just delivered everything else."

"Then it sounds like all we need is our guest of honor."

Grace hiked her day bag up on her shoulder and headed toward the employee lounge to unload and grab a cup of coffee.

She'd passed her mother as she was finalizing the arrangement for Mr. Kurtz that had just arrived. Grace prepared herself a cup of coffee and then went to put the final preparations on Mr. Kurtz.

His casket was open, and her brother had set the box of personal items on the table for her to attend to. Inside were his glasses, which the family had asked him to wear, his wedding band, and a Navy pin for his lapel.

"Good morning, Mr. Kurtz. It looks as though everything is in order for you this morning."

She took his glasses out and set them on his face. It was a wonder what a difference glasses made, even when the person's eyes were closed.

With care, she placed the pin on the lapel of his jacket. "Thank you for your service," she said and wondered if he was going to speak to her, but he didn't.

Lastly, she managed on his wedding band.

"You're all set, Mr. Kurtz. Is there anything else I can do for you?"

There was nothing. The air in the room didn't stir. There were no whispers—no chills.

It was a strange feeling to hope that she hadn't angered him when they'd used him to talk to Nora, but perhaps they had.

"I'm going to take you into the chapel now. Your family will be arriving shortly."

Just as she unlocked the wheels on the cart that carried the casket, she was hit in the chest with a sharp blast of cold so intense it threw her backward and into the counter.

Grace fought to catch her breath, which now escaped in a cloud of mist before her.

She'd never had something like that happen, but she didn't think it was Mr. Kurtz that had done it to her. Pressing her hand to her chest, she tried to breathe through the pain of it. As she took in deep breaths, she could smell dirt—wet dirt.

The scent made her cough, and when her brother walked through the door, she jumped, startled by his presence.

"Are you okay? I heard a crash in here."

She collected herself. "I must have lost my footing. I unlocked the cart and fell back against the counter."

"Are you okay? Your cheeks are red, and you look like you scratched yourself. You're bleeding."

Grace looked down at her hand that she'd pressed to her chest. Sure enough, there was a small trace of blood.

"I'm fine though. I guess I did scratch myself."

Scott nodded as he scanned a look over her. "I'll take him to the chapel. You pull yourself together. His family will be here in ten minutes."

"I'll be fine." She smiled but wondered if it actually surfaced in her eyes by the way her brother stared at her.

Scott opened the wide door and pushed Mr. Kurtz out of the room. Grace stood there, leaning up against the counter, and looking at the blood on her hand.

She wasn't stupid enough to think that she'd just fallen over and scratched herself. And she wasn't foolish enough to believe that this curse that she possessed, talking to the deceased, was only for good people. Darkness most certainly could cloud her interceptions. What she didn't understand was why. Why would anyone in her realm, or any other realm, want to hurt her?

Grace's phone buzzed in the pocket of her jacket. She pulled it out to see a text message from Matthew. *I talked to the gentlemen, and we're going to film right before first pitch on Saturday. Wear your game gear.*

She smiled down at the phone and thought of the good they were going to do with this power that she had. Therefore, there was no need to think something dangerous could come through and get her.

Her phone chimed again, and she looked down at the next text. *I love you.*

Quickly the scratch on her chest and the stabbing cold that had hit her were a memory. She warmed from the top of her head to the tips of her toes when she read his words. He did love her. She knew that as sure as she knew her own name.

Grace typed back. *I love you too.*

Tucking her phone back in her pocket, she wondered what Matthew would think of the events that had unfolded that morning. Coincidence, that was all. Mr. Kurtz was done talking to people on their side, and she had lost her balance. Seriously, she'd be equally as foolish to not consider that those were the circumstances.

Grace turned off the lights and left the room.

With a stop by the bathroom, she tended to the scratch across her chest, just under her neck. It was too high to cover with her blouse, but she thought she might have a scarf in her bag. She always carried one, just in case she spilled on her suit.

Just as she turned to leave the bathroom, the lights flickered, and again she could smell fresh soil.

She rubbed her nose as the lights came back on. The scent lingered, and she caught herself wincing at the smell in the mirror.

In the small cabinet in the corner was a bottle of air freshener. She took the liberty of dousing the small bathroom with the spray in hopes that no one else would smell that earthy scent.

THE SERVICE for Mr. Kurtz was as lovely as they had planned. Grace was pleased to hear the kind words that were spoken about him.

During the service, she and Scott closed the casket, and she heard the whisper.

Be careful. I didn't do that to you.

As the lid closed, Scott adjusted the spray and took Grace by the elbow to the back of the chapel for the continuation of the service.

Again, the air chilled around her, and she could smell earth, only now it choked her. She excused herself to the employee lounge where she coughed until she made herself throw up what was left of her breakfast in the trash can by the sink.

Pulling down a glass, she filled it with water from the sink and drank it down. Trying to rid herself of the taste of dirt, she rinsed her mouth and spat out the water.

When the door opened, her mother ran to her side. "Are you okay? You're pale. You're sweating."

"I'm fine. I don't know what..."

"You've been throwing up. We need to get you home."

"Mom, I'm fine. I think I just ate something that didn't agree with me," Grace argued as she pulled on the scarf she'd tied on, and now seemed to be choking her.

"Oh, God, Grace. What happened to you?"

Her mother tugged off the scarf and shook her head. "I've seen this before. You need to go home. You need to stay home."

"You've seen what? I don't understand."

Her mother's eyes grew wide with worry. "You're communicating with the deceased has opened you up. Someone is trying to get to you—trying to show you something or hurt you. You need to get out of here."

For the very first time in her life, Grace was afraid of the *gift* she possessed.

Nodding, she turned to her locker and pulled out her bag. All she wanted was to get away from the mortuary, and death, as quickly as she could.

CHAPTER 29

*M*atthew's knuckles were raw from knocking on Grace's door. The phone call that had come from her mother had him terrified especially after all the texts he'd received from Rebecca.

The moment she opened her front door, Matthew pulled Grace into his arms and kissed her head, her face, her cheek.

"God, I was so worried about you. Your mother scared me to death."

Grace pulled back and looked up at him. "My mother called you?"

"Yes. She said they couldn't get away from the mortuary, but that something had happened to you, and that you were sick." He stopped when he noticed the gash on her chest, just under her throat. "Grace, what happened to you?" he asked as he went to touch her skin, and then pulled back. "What did you do?"

Grace shoved away from him and walked toward her kitchen. "What did I do? You think I did that to myself?"

"I didn't mean it that..."

"Sure you did. You don't know me. You don't

know what I go through." She pulled a bottle of water from the refrigerator, opened it, and took a long drink. "I'm sure my mother didn't tell you I was attacked by some spirit. Right?"

Matthew's mouth went dry. "You were attacked by a spirit?"

"Sounds stupid, right? Crazy Grace, making crap up again."

"Whoa." He moved to her and took the bottle from her hands. Setting it on the counter, he turned back and placed his hands on her shoulders. "Don't go labeling me as some regular person. That's not going to fly. I'm not calling you crazy. I've just never been around anyone who was attacked like this. Now let's just sit down, talk it out, and figure out what we need to do."

"What we need to do?"

"Yes. We. You and me. Grace, we're a team. Don't cut me off now."

Her shoulders dropped, and she fell against him, her cheek pressed to his chest.

"I don't know what happened. I went to get Mr. Kurtz ready for his funeral, and I was talking to him. I really wanted to apologize for using him the other day, but he wouldn't talk back to me." She eased back. "I suppose the deceased could be mad too."

Grace picked back up the water and took another drink. "He wouldn't talk. I figured maybe he'd crossed over. But while I was standing there, something struck me. It felt like someone had stabbed me with an icicle."

"That's what happened to your neck?"

Grace nodded and drank again. "Then I could smell dirt. Fresh dirt. Dirt that had just been turned over."

"Damp, not dusty?"

Her eyes opened wide. "Yes."

"Do you think someone is trying to signal you?"

"Yes, but it doesn't make sense. Why hurt me?"

"And you don't think it was Mr. Kurtz?"

"No, because at his funeral, when we closed his casket, he told me to be careful and that he hadn't done this to me. I'm not doing anything wrong with this power. I'm setting out to do good with it."

Matthew took her hand and kissed her fingers. "I know. I know." He pulled her in close again. "Your mom wants you to take a few days off. So, I'm going to go back to work for a few hours and get my segments finished up. Then the only thing I'll have left on my agenda is recording with the men in the cemetery on Saturday. And you can go, but only if you feel up to it."

"I'll be fine."

"I'm sure you will be." He kissed the top of her head. "This is all new to me, Grace. Work me into it, okay? Understand that everything you tell me is going to be new to me. But I'm not going anywhere. I know you talked to my grandmother. I know when she's around now, and I talk to her myself. She doesn't talk back, but I know she hears me. I want to be a part of all of this."

Grace eased back. "You want to help me with last goodbyes?"

"I do. Who knows, maybe there are a few good stories out there."

"Ah..." she teased as she hugged him tightly. "I have one more to check off the list on Saturday."

"What's that?"

"On Mrs. Rodriguez's list, she wanted her husband to find someone new."

"And you're going to facilitate that?"

"I am. Remember Mrs. Fallon from the river walk?"

"Cancer support group woman."

"That's her. I'm going to set them up."

"And you think he'll go for that?"

"Oh, I think it'll work itself out. I just have to give him her card."

Matthew gave her a squeeze back. "I love how you think."

* * *

THE DRIVE back to the station was a long one. Matthew hadn't been so freaked out and worried about another person in a very long time. Something —someone had set out to hurt Grace, but why? Were they mad at her for messing around in another realm? She'd said Mr. Kurtz told her he hadn't attacked her but was that true? He'd have a reason, Matthew thought.

Matthew focused on his segments for Friday morning. They weren't running anything but a few promos, and he was grateful for that. He did have to get some work done on another segment that would air on Monday, and of course, figure out what the hell he was going to ask the men at the cemetery tomorrow, but he figured that would be organic.

What he really wanted to do was to tell Kyle to make it all look good, and he wanted to get back to Grace.

While Kyle was busy editing, Matthew took a few moments to look up the paranormal. There were so many ways people claimed to interact with spirits. He'd seen a few instances where they communicated in the same way Grace did. Some people meditated on it, others, like Grace, just had it happen.

He searched for scents, as he'd encountered with his grandmother, or so Grace had told him. He found that when a certain scent surrounded a person, it often meant that a spirit was near. In this case, it was very specific to his grandmother.

But Grace was smelling earth. What did that mean?

Kyle gave himself a little cheer when he created the lead in for Matthew's segment, and he gave him a thumbs up, then went back to his research when his phone chimed in his pocket. He pulled it out and saw that there was another text message from Rebecca.

Seriously, he'd had enough. It was time to tell her to leave him alone.

When he opened the message, he saw that there were empty text bubbles—fifteen he counted.

What in the world was she doing? This had gone too far.

Matthew began to type a new text to her when his phone screen went blank and a crack formed on his screen.

"What in the hell?" He dropped it to the desk as he watched the glass shatter.

"Dude, that's expensive."

"I didn't drop it. It's self-destructing," Matthew said as he picked up the phone and dropped it back down because it was so hot it burned his fingers.

"Whoa." Kyle moved in closer. "Big brother is watching and destroying."

The sickness of panic spread through Matthew's chest. "I've got to get home. Are we good here?"

"Yeah, man. Go. They'll have what they need, and I'll meet you at the cemetery on Saturday morning."

"Perfect." Matthew gathered his keys, leaving his phone on the desk, and hurried out to his car. It had to be a coincidence that his phone had just exploded in his hand on the same day that something attacked Grace. He wasn't connected to the other side. No one should be trying to contact him or hurt him. And not once had he smelled roses, which meant that it wasn't a sign from his grandmother.

As he sped out of the parking lot, all he could think about was getting to Grace. Hopefully, the strange phenomenon was isolated to that day, because he wasn't sure how much more he could take.

CHAPTER 30

*W*ithout his phone chiming or ringing in his pocket, Matthew thought the evening and next day were peaceful. Of course, not having his phone caused him to call into the station multiple times just to check in.

He hadn't divulged precisely what had happened when his phone exploded in his hand, because he wasn't exactly sure himself. The thought that he should reach out to Rebecca had crossed his mind, but he was still angry at her for how she behaved that morning at his house. And the more he thought about it, the angrier he got.

Fine, he hadn't handled his grief well enough to just tell her he needed his space. He ate the food she offered. He'd taken the comfort she'd given. And, damnit, he'd kissed her and let her sleep in his bed. Though he might be mad at Rebecca for it all, he was the fool.

Grace tapped him on the thigh as they watched a movie propped up with a million pillows on her bed since it was the only TV she had in the house.

"You're a million miles away," she asked, and he tore himself from his thoughts and looked at her.

God, she was beautiful. He found himself thanking his grandmother every day for somehow throwing them into one another's path.

"Yeah." He kissed the top of her head. "I'm fine. Just not used to sitting around," he said and actually thought she believed it.

"We don't just have to sit around the house. I'm just staying away from the mortuary. We have all afternoon. We could go to a movie, walk the river, or just get some ice cream."

"Ice cream? Let me guess, you're a strawberry kind of girl."

She winced. "Allergic to strawberries."

"That's a good one to know. I won't be giving you any for Valentine's day then. Anything else?"

"Nope, just strawberries. You?"

"I don't care for yogurt. Not allergic to it, but I just don't understand the fascination with curdled milk."

Grace snorted out a laugh. "I won't serve that for your breakfast then."

"Why don't we take a little hike. Just up Johnson's trail. It's not steep, it's shaded, but we can get out in nature."

"I like it. Let me find my shoes."

Matthew watched her climb off the bed and go to her closet. He wondered if he would ever tire watching her do the most mundane things. He'd found great joy in just watching her brush her teeth that morning. Love—who would have thought it would have struck him as it had?

* * *

GRACE HAD NEVER ACTUALLY HIKED Johnson's trail.

She knew the kids in high school used to meet up there for bonfires and beer, but she didn't run that way. She was more likely to meet a group of friends at the movies and then hang out at someone's house. Hiking up a hill to drink, and then getting back down the hill only brought on bad things. Jeremy Tank had broken his wrist and his ankle one night trying to get off the side of the mountain. And she remembered that Kelly Simmons cracked her head open. Of course, there were always the rumors that no one hiked alone because someone would carry you off into the woods.

Grace always thought that was common sense more than anything. Seriously, why would someone hike alone, especially a woman? Perhaps she just wasn't a strong enough personality to even consider such a thing.

"Have you hiked up here a lot?" she asked Matthew as they parked in the lot at the base of the trail.

"I would run the trail training for races."

"That's right. You're a runner."

"Was. Tore my ACL, surgery, recovery, and all. Decided then that it wasn't worth my time. I haven't been up here in years, but the thought just popped in my head that this would be a good spot to get out of the house," he said on a laugh as he put the car in park, and they climbed out.

Grace had slathered on sunscreen before leaving the house and had taken a lot of pleasure in doing the same to Matthew. She'd packed them a small lunch and put it in her backpack, which she flung onto her back.

As she skirted the front of the car, she noticed Matthew scanning the parking lot. "What are you looking for?"

"Just thought I recognized a car," he said before turning and sliding on his sunglasses. "Ready?"

They took off for the trail in the July heat. Grace was grateful for the shade that the trees lining the path had provided. She enjoyed a good walk, but she never was one to just take off and hike, though she'd always wanted to. Perhaps this would be something new that she and Matthew could do together. After all, wasn't that the joy in having someone in your life? It was a chance to share new opportunities.

Thirty minutes into their hike, Matthew suggested that they sit down on a large boulder and hydrate. Grace pulled out a bag of apple slices and offered him some.

"Maybe it was too hot to do this today," she suggested.

"We did just half-ass it," he admitted. "We should have planned a little better and taken off earlier."

"I think I'd like to do this again."

"We'll make a plan then. There's a lot of great trails around here."

They sipped their water and ate their apples. Unanimously, they decided to turn back for the car.

As Grace swung the backpack over her shoulder, her vision blurred, and she swayed. The smell of fresh earth again penetrated her nose, and she felt the rise of sickness move from her stomach to her throat. The sensation of her knees giving out on her was the last thing she remembered, and then everything went to black.

MATTHEW WATCHED as Grace started to fall toward the boulder. Her eyes had rolled back, and as he caught her, they both fell to the ground, luckily missing the boulder.

"Grace. Grace!" he shouted, and she moaned in his arms. "God, what the hell happened? Grace, can you hear me?"

She moaned again before opening her eyes and looking up at him. For a moment it looked as though she were unclear of who he was, then she blinked and came around.

"Are you trying to give me a heart attack out here?" he scolded. "I told you to drink water."

"I did. I was." Grace struggled to sit up, and he helped her to a seated position in the dirt. "That was weird."

"Weird? That was terrifying."

"My head started to spin, and I felt sick. Then I could smell dirt again, just like the other day at the mortuary."

Matthew felt the blood drain from his face. "It's following you?"

"What?"

"Whatever attacked you at the mortuary. And I'm not comforted that you don't hear my grandmother or smell her."

"I'm sure it was the elevation. And I'm surrounded by dirt," she pointed out. "I just got..." she stopped talking and closed her eyes.

"Don't do this again," he warned.

"Wilting roses. Don't you smell it?"

"Let's get you back to the car."

"You don't?"

"No. And I'm scared to death and freaking out. Grace, let's go. Can you walk?"

She got to her feet. "I'm fine. If someone is trying to communicate with me, they'd better try a new tactic. This one is inconvenient."

Grace started back down the trail, and Matthew

hurried to catch up with her. "Inconvenient? That's all you have to say?"

"I don't know what more to say. This is new to me, but so was the very first time I heard someone in a casket talk to me. In time, I'll get it figured out."

"I worry that there isn't going to be more time. If this keeps attacking you…"

"I'll block it."

"How?"

"I don't know. It'll need more than earphones, but I'll learn to block it."

"Wilting roses, what does that mean?"

"I'd tell you if I knew," she said as she continued to walk at a faster pace than he was comfortable with. "I assume it was your grandmother sending some kind of signal. What kind, I don't know. Maybe I can get her to talk to me tomorrow."

He reached for her arm and stopped her. "You're not going into the mortuary tomorrow."

"Like hell, I'm not. It's as much my home as my home," she argued. "I'll just get her to talk through someone, and we can ask some questions."

"I don't like this."

"You keep saying that, and I don't see it getting us any closer to an answer. This is the only way we're going to figure it out."

Matthew pursed his lips. "I love you, so I need to know, are you always this stubborn?"

"I suppose you should ask my family that question. As far as I'm concerned, I'm the only one with the ability to ask the other side what's happening."

Matthew gritted his teeth and groaned. "Okay, but you let me be with you, or at least close enough to get to you. You were attacked, and I have no doubt it was from a spirit that didn't like you meddling in something."

"Ah, you want to protect me."

"Don't joke, Grace. I want to protect you. And I want to talk to you in this realm and not have to wait until I smell your scent to know you're lingering around."

"I get it," she said softly. "I'll be careful. I can smell her roses now. It's not wilting either."

He focused on the air around him. "It's faint."

"But it's there."

"She's going to see us off this trail."

"She's looking out for us," Grace confirmed.

"Good. Let's get home."

CHAPTER 31

$\mathcal{C}$ell phones were not that difficult, Matthew thought as he pressed the numbers on the phone that the station had given him. When his other phone had exploded, he lost all of his contacts. Luckily, some of them had been backed up to his computer.

Grace sat on the edge of his desk at the station and fidgeted with the knickknacks he kept on the shelf above his computer screen.

"I don't understand this," she said as she shook the snow globe. "This is from the Caribbean. It has Santa it in a swimsuit. Why does it need snow?"

Matthew took the snow glove from her and placed it back on the shelf, just as he would a small child playing with something they weren't supposed to touch. "Knickknacks don't have any purpose. I'm not even sure why I have all of this on my desk."

He punched in a few more numbers on the cell phone and realized his attitude was not going to help him when they went to film at the cemetery. But then again, that was what was bothering him. He didn't want Grace anywhere near the cemetery, and he didn't want to tell her.

"If you didn't like knickknacks, why do you have so many of them?" Grace asked as she picked up a pen with a small ship that would go from end to end as she tilted the pen.

"It just happens. People bring this crap, and I put it on my desk."

Grace put the pen back and stood next to him. "Is there a lounge or lobby? I think you would feel better if I got out of your way."

Matthew put the phone down on the top of his desk and pulled her to him. "I'm sorry. I have a lot on my mind, and I'm taking it out on you."

"What's bothering you?"

Matthew sucked in a deep breath. "Honestly? I'm worried about you going to the cemetery. I don't know what attacked you at the mortuary. I don't know what happened to you on the trail. Grace, I don't want anything to happen to you again."

She smiled down at him, almost angelic. "I don't want it to happen again either, but I need to face. My mother said she'd seen it before. She didn't say anything else, and that would've been helpful. But if it has happened before, then somebody knows how to deal with it."

Matthew nodded. "You're right. Maybe after we talk to the gentleman in the cemetery, we can sit down with your parents and ask some questions."

He saw the flashing disapproval in her eyes, but the smile on her lips said that she would agree. All he knew, was that he never wanted her hurt again. And he never wanted to see what he saw on that trail either.

As Grace stepped back, the phone on Matthew's desk began to chime over and over again. He picked it up and looked at it.

Grace leaned in over his shoulder. "Is somebody already texting you?"

"It's the same phone number I had. These are probably texts that never went through."

"They're all the same number."

Matthew bit down on his lip. "They're all from Rebecca."

Grace eased back. "Oh. What did she have to say?"

He held up the phone so that she could see the screen. "They're empty. After she texted me this enormous rant, then I just started to get empty texts."

"And that's why you got a new phone? The text messages weren't working?"

He set the phone back on his desk and turned to her. "I didn't want to say anything, but now I think everything fits together. I didn't break the phone, it exploded in my hands."

Grace licked her lips in a way that told him her mouth had gone dry. "It just exploded in your hands?"

"The text messages are blank, and the phone self-destructed. I'm not making it up."

Grace touched the scratch on her neck. "I get it. I was thrown across the room by an angry spirit, re-member? You can talk all the crazy to me you want. I'm apt to buy into it."

"I've never had anything like this happen to me. If it weren't for the fact that I can sometimes smell roses and you told me things that only my grand-mother could have told you, I'd think I was going crazy. But..." He picked up the new phone and looked down at the blank text messages. "Someone is trying awfully hard to get a message through to us."

"Do you think they're trying to stop us from someone's last goodbye?"

Matthew shrugged. "I don't know why they're just not telling you that then."

"My mom said she'd seen something like this before," she offered tapping the scratch on her neck. "Maybe she can enlighten us."

"Maybe. I'm going to call Rebecca and just make sure everything is okay."

Grace's eyes were soft as she watched him. "I wouldn't expect anything less. She's your friend. If someone is trying to get a message to us, why use her name?"

"Because I'd notice."

"There's that. But you should make sure she's okay."

Matthew nodded as he looked down at the phone.

Grace placed a kiss on the top of his head. "I'm going to use the restroom. You take a few minutes to talk to her."

He watched as she turned and walked down the hallway before he began his message to Rebecca.

Are you OK? I keep getting weird messages from you.

He waited, and again the bubbles popped up as if she were replying, and then the texts scrolled up and were empty.

Something must be wrong with her phone, he decided. It didn't make sense that for two days, and two phones, he was getting the same things popping up.

Matthew hit the call button and waited for Rebecca to answer the phone. After four rings it sounded as if the line had been picked up before it went silent.

Leaning back in his chair, he thought about how angry she was when he'd seen her last. No doubt she was hanging up on him. But then he thought about the parking lot when they'd gone for their hike earlier. Matthew was sure he'd seen her car. Could she have been following them?

He chuckled at the thought. Rebecca wouldn't be

caught dead in hiking boots or sneakers for that matter. There was no way the car he'd seen was hers. She might be mad, but even she wouldn't climb up the side of a mountain just to spy on him.

Sliding the phone into his pocket, he looked up to see Kyle crossing the room.

"I'm loaded and ready to go. Are you driving over with me?" he asked as he took a long drink from his Red Bull can.

"I'll drive over with Grace. Follow us in from the gate, and we'll head over to the section where the men meet up."

"That's some crazy stuff, hanging out in a cemetery and listening to a ball game."

"It's sweet," Matthew offered as he turned off his computer screen. "Can you imagine loving someone so much that even when one of you is gone you still sit with them? And to make it a block party..."

"That's weird," Kyle said as he took another drink and then let out a long burp.

Matthew watched as Kyle crushed the can and gave it his best free throw toss into the trash. Yeah, Kyle might never find true love and understand what it meant, but Matthew was very sure that's what he'd found just over a week ago with Grace. And all he could think was, thank God for that.

CHAPTER 32

*K*yle set the camera up just beyond where the men sat with their table between them and the radio that played the game. They'd quickly offered Matthew a beer, but he told them he'd take them up on it when they were done filming the segment.

Mr. Leeds had even brought Grace a chair, and one of those little bottles of wine. She sat off to the side, a grin on her lips, and watched as Matthew situated himself and coordinated with Kyle.

"I want this to be just friendly banter," Matthew said as he fixed Mr. Rodriguez's microphone on his lapel. "I'm going to ask you a few questions, but feel free to talk as we did the other day. If you have something to say, a story to share, a joke, whatever, just say it."

"Will we be done before the third inning? I don't want to miss too much of the game," Mr. Leeds asked.

"We will make it short and sweet. I promise," Matthew stepped back and gave Kyle a nod to confirm that he was recording.

The men began to talk to one another, as Matthew assumed they did each time they met. They were fortunate to have built such a friendship from something that could have torn them apart as individuals.

"When did the two of you decide to bring in the chairs and the radio?" Matthew asked as he stood next to Kyle.

Mr. Rodriguez, legs crossed, bounced his foot as he thought. "I think my wife was buried here in March and his wife mid-April."

"Yup," Mr. Leeds confirmed.

"At the time I had an old Home Depot bucket in the back of my car that I'd haul over here and sit on so I could talk to my wife. I wasn't very independent then, and I was mad that my socks had turned pink when I washed them."

Mr. Leeds laughed at his friend's memory, but sat quietly, his hands both cupped around his beer as Mr. Rodriguez continued.

"For the first few weeks, we'd see each other and acknowledge one another with a nod. When you're that lonely, and you miss your wife so much, you don't want to talk to others."

"But that changed?" Matthew prompted.

"One afternoon he and his daughter were sitting here, each had chairs like we do now. His daughter asked me about my ball cap, and she and I talked baseball. He," he nodded toward Mr. Leeds, "sat there without a word to say."

"She broke the ice?"

"Yeah. They were there the next day, only they had three chairs. She'd brought an extra just in case I might come by."

"Thoughtful."

"Sure was. We discussed the game we'd all just watched on TV before heading out to the cemetery.

She suggested we meet up the next day to listen to the game, and that's what we did."

Mr. Leeds tipped up his cap, and Matthew noted that he wiped his fingers under his glasses. "She got us talking and then flew back to Ohio the next week."

"And the two of you have been sharing games ever since?"

They both nodded.

Mr. Rodriguez took a sip from his beer. "It's good to share with others. His wife was much older than mine. Mine was taking in her prime. He helped me through that."

It was the first time that Matthew noticed the twenty years that Mr. Leeds had on Mr. Rodriguez.

"Do you keep up with each other away from the cemetery?"

Mr. Rodriguez began bouncing his foot again. "After about two years we did. His family invited me for Thanksgiving—the same daughter that got us talking. Now we check in on each other during the offseason if we don't see each other. We text dirty jokes to each other too."

Mr. Leeds laughed but bowed his head, and Matthew was quite sure he was the instigator of that.

"It's a good friendship," Mr. Rodriguez continued. "I'd like to have sat and listened to ball games much earlier on our back porches. This isn't really the place you want to meet people, but death brings the living together. And we're all grateful for little Grace over there who helped to make the transition easier."

Kyle turned his camera to capture Grace who sat in the sun, her mini bottle of wine in her hands, and a huge smile that pushed up her sunglasses high on her cheeks.

Wasn't it amazing? Death had led Matthew to Grace too. They were all thankful for that.

Each of the men told stories about their wives. Mr. Leeds and his wife had been sweethearts since they were young, having grown up in a small farming town. Matthew wondered if Mrs. Leeds was as quietly spoken as her husband, or if she were the center of attention.

The stories Mr. Rodriguez shared of his wife were similar in tone. He missed her terribly, and the love for her still resonated from his eyes. "Cancer sucks," he said as he wiped a tear from his eye. "We had a lot of plans left. I've got my kids, but they're grown and have families of their own. My wife and I were supposed to grow old together, not just gray." He weakly chuckled at his own joke, and Matthew caught a glimpse of Grace, from the corner of his eye, wiping away a tear too.

Once the men were more engaged in their ball game than the interview, Kyle took some surrounding shots of the cemetery and closeups of the headstones of Mrs. Leeds and Mrs. Rodriguez. Then he shook hands with the gentlemen and headed back to the station.

"I appreciate you both sharing some more time with me," Matthew said as he shook each of the gentlemen's hands.

"Our pleasure. I'll get a load of crap about it when it airs from the guys at the Elks, but it's worth it," Mr. Rodriguez replaced his ball cap on his head. "Eh, I hope we don't end up with a hundred people sitting out here with us next weekend." He laughed, and so did Mr. Leeds.

"That would be a sight," Matthew said as Grace walked up beside him.

"Darling, if this boy ever treats you wrong, you let us know," Mr. Rodriguez said with a nod in Matthew's direction. "You deserve only the best."

She smiled up at Matthew. "He's doing a fine job so far. Oh," she said as she reached her hand into her purse. "I have something I wanted to give you."

"Give me?"

"Yes." She pulled out the business card from the woman they'd met in the park on the fourth of July.

"Cancer spouse support?" He looked up at Grace, his brows drawn together. "It's been a few years."

"I know. Mrs. Fallon was one of our families here a few years ago, and I thought of you when I spoke to her the other day. I know that grief never goes away, and I thought it would be a good resource for you."

Mr. Rodriguez wrinkled up his nose and puckered his lips as he slipped the card into his breast pocket. "Thanks."

Matthew wasn't sure the warmth was behind his gratitude. This last goodbye item might need more work than just that, but Grace had taken the first step.

"I think we'll let you get back to your game," Matthew said just as Mr. Leeds reached for Grace's hand.

"What happened to you?" he asked.

Matthew saw the flash of shock register on Grace's face before she masked it with a smile. She reached her hand to her neck.

"I fell while moving a casket," she said. "I lost my balance after I unlocked the cart."

Mr. Leeds nodded slowly. "I hope you're okay." His worry was also replaced with a friendly smile that didn't quite reach his eyes.

They said goodbye to the gentlemen and headed back toward Matthew's car.

"I should have covered that up," Grace whispered to him.

"I'll be honest. I didn't think about it this morning because it had faded, but it looks fresh again."

When they reached his car, Grace slid in and opened the mirror on the back of the sunshade.

"What the heck?" She examined it as Matthew climbed into the car. "This is what it looked like right after it happened."

"I think we should take you to a doctor."

She shook her head. "No." A moment later she coughed and her eyes watered. "I smell dirt again."

"Let's get you out of here. You're too close."

Grace rested her hand on his as he gripped the steering wheel. "No. I need to go inside."

"I'm not letting you go into the mortuary. It's too dangerous."

"Go with me. Someone is trying to tell me something. This is the only way I'm going to face it."

He hated the very thought of her suggestion, but he knew she was right. Grace needed to face the spirit that was harming her, no matter how horrible an idea it was.

Matthew drove through the cemetery toward the mortuary as Grace continued to cough.

CHAPTER 33

*W*orking to stay calm, Grace breathed in slowly, but her nose and throat filled with the taste of dirt.

She didn't want Matthew to worry, but she could see the panic in his eyes. Opening her purse for a tissue, she noticed the safe combination which Mr. Jackson had given her years ago. She'd slid it into her purse so that she could look up the address. She wasn't sure what she was going to do, but she owed it to Mr. Jackson to get that piece of paper to his wife.

Finally, she found a tissue buried in the bottom of her purse. Dabbing her eyes, she noticed Matthew watching her from the corner of his as he pulled into the parking lot and parked the car.

"I'm still not sure about this," he said as he turned off the engine. "You look as if you need a doctor and not a conversation with a dead person."

"Deceased," she corrected.

"Same," he grunted. "Now what?"

"Now I go inside and see who has arrived and try to communicate with someone."

"Just anyone?"

"I don't have many choices here."

"And your mother is going to let you do that?"

Grace shoved the tissue back into her purse. "My mother will understand. Everyone in my family will understand."

"But will they want you to do this? Look at you. You can't breathe, and that scratch on your neck looks horrible."

Grace pulled the scarf that she kept in her purse out and wrapped it around her neck. "All better," she said as she opened the door and stepped out of the car.

Without looking back, she walked briskly toward the building, afraid that Matthew might stop her.

As she pulled open the door to the building that same mighty cold that had knocked her across the room and scratched her, knocked her back, throwing her to the ground.

She heard Matthew yell for her, and then her mother and father's voices filled her ears.

"I'm fine. I'm fine!" she shouted as she sat up, her head throbbing from hitting the ground.

"Grace, what happened?" Her mother's voice had risen two octaves.

She shifted a glare toward Matthew who had knelt down next to her. Her mother reached her hand toward Grace's neck. "You were attacked again," her voice was a whisper.

"Again?" Her father knelt down next to her now. "Grace, what's going on?"

Grace rubbed her hand over the bump on the back of her head. "It's nothing I can't handle."

"You don't know that," her mother warned.

Grace looked up at her father. "Someone is trying to tell me something, only their tactic is a bit disruptive."

"Disruptive?" he repeated his word, just as

Matthew had done on the trail. "They did that to your neck and threw you out the door? I'd say it's more than disruptive." He stood and raked his fingers through his hair. "I saw this happen to my mother. Grace, I don't want you to be part of this."

"I think it's a little late, and had I known this was dangerous, I wouldn't have come back to work here years ago, but no one mentioned this part," she said with a bite.

She watched her father chew on his bottom lip as he considered his next words. "Why did you stop wearing the headphones?"

Matthew took hold of her hand. "My grandmother got through to her," he admitted as he pressed a kiss to her scuffed knuckles. "My grandmother has convinced her to pass on final goodbye wishes."

Her father scrubbed his hands over his face. "Let's go inside and talk about this."

Matthew shook his head. "I don't think that's safe."

Grace watched her father close his eyes and lift his head. A moment later he opened his eyes and looked at her. "It's safe. Let's go."

Grace studied him. What had he just done? What had he just seen? Her father had never done something like that, nor would he take her somewhere she might be hurt. Did he hear voices too?

Matthew got to his feet and helped Grace up. They followed her parents into the mortuary and back to the employee lounge, past Ella Walsh who had stood to hurry to them but was called off by a gentle nod by her father.

When she sat in the lounge, her mother closed and locked the door as her father filled her a glass of water.

"Are you mad?" she asked as he handed there the glass and she took a sip.

"No. How could I be mad? If it weren't his grandmother asking you to do this, it would have been my mother asking. I would have told Nora Campbell the same thing I told my mother, and that is that if you let in all the spirts that want to talk to you, you're going to let in a few bad ones too."

"That's what I'm afraid of," Matthew said, his arms crossed over his chest and a mix of panic and anger shifting in his eyes.

Grace's father took the seat next to her. "I assume that everything has been relatively calm until recently? And considering Nora Campbell only passed a few weeks ago, this is a new quest?"

"Yes."

"Okay then, we need to figure out how to handle the bad spirits that come to talk. They have things to say too, and they need their goodbyes too, I suppose."

"But what if those goodbyes are supposed to hurt someone?"

"Then you do as you've always done. You ignore them."

Matthew moved toward the table. "But will they listen? Did this only happen because she was hearing them? If she ignored them, they'd go away?"

Her father acknowledged Matthew with a slight nod. "She's warded them off for years and didn't even know it."

Grace felt her mouth fall open as she gasped at her father's words. "You've heard them the whole time?"

"I hear parts," he admitted. "I can't hear what you or my mother heard. I can't have conversations, but I can feel the energy around me. I knew when Nora was in our care that she would be very important to you." Matthew rested his hand on Grace's shoulder, and her father smiled. "If there is a need to finish business on earth, then I guess you have a job."

"Beth Cartwright came to us because she was told I could talk to her mother and have her wishes passed along. Is that normal?"

"Those who are receptive to you, here on earth and in other realms, will use you. Such as Mrs. Cartwright's wishes. Her daughter must be open to someone who passed on that information."

"Great. I'm part of a Google search in another realm."

Her father laughed now and the seriousness slipped from his eyes. "Don't do this, Grace, if you don't want to. No one is keeping you here."

She felt Matthew's fingers squeeze her shoulder in support. "I need to do this. I feel as if I need to do this."

Her father lifted his eyes to Matthew. "And you? What do you think of all of this?"

"It's new to me. But Grace has offered me proof that my Grandmother is there watching over us and communicating with her. I think she has a lot to offer to those who have passed and those who must live on."

Grace reached for her father's hand. "Did Grandma talk to those she cared for? Did she pass on last goodbyes?"

A smile formed on her father's lips as he placed his other hand atop hers. "She tried. Some were receptive, and some weren't, but she tried. I think the older she got it was too much, but being the last person that someone communicated with on earth was a big responsibility to her and a great honor. I know she'd be proud of you to take that on."

"And what about you, Dad?"

"Like I said, it's a big responsibility and a great honor. I wouldn't judge you if you walked away from it. I know what a burden it is to hear what you hear. But, Grace, imagine the comfort you could bring to others."

She thought about the lipstick Mrs. Gordon had wanted to wear, the words Grace had passed on to the daughters of the young mother she'd cared for, and of course Mrs. Cartwright's last wishes being honored. These were things she'd facilitated, as well as *setting up* Mr. Rodriguez by handing him the business card for Mrs. Fallon. Then she thought of the troublesome spirit that kept hurting her. Were they trying to get her attention to warn her away from something, or guide her toward something? Was she so frightened that she hadn't been paying attention? And why did Nora not talk to her when this other spirit was trying to get through?

Swallowing hard, Grace looked into her father's eyes and smiled. "It would be an honor to follow in Grandma's footsteps and bring peace and comfort to families who need it."

"She always knew you would feel that way, Grace. She knew what a burden it was to pass this gift to you, but she also knew you would find good in it."

"What about Scott? Can he hear them?"

Her father chuckled. "He can't even hear his own thoughts." He patted her hand again. "He's good at what he does. This gift is your gift. Go home. Rest. Maybe on Monday, we can find someone who can tell you what's going on."

By finding someone, she knew he meant that a new person would be there for her to work on, and it would mean going back to work and back to normal.

Her father kissed her cheek as he stood from the table and left the room with her mother.

"I guess my business card now says *final giver of goodbyes*."

Matthew pressed a kiss to the top of her head. "I can't think of anyone who would be better for the job. Let's go home and relax. It sounds like next week might get more interesting than today."

CHAPTER 34

*T*here was an energy that buzzed through Grace, which both thrilled and terrified her. Getting Matthew's family to plant a rose bush in a granddaughter's back yard was an easy task. Making sure that a lipstick shade was worn into eternity, that too was no problem. But the air around Grace stirred differently now. There was unease in the whispers she heard on the air, and her attention was being pulled from the usual tasks of relaxation on a Sunday morning to needing to do something to find calm in her heart.

Matthew sat at her kitchen table in his lounge pants and a T-shirt thumbing through the newspaper that had landed on her front step that morning. He'd absentmindedly reach for his cup of coffee and take a sip, all without moving the paper at all.

Grace wondered how much of this was an act, a slight tactic to act as if he were ignoring her so that she wouldn't want to run off somewhere, but that was only making her more fidgety.

"Maybe we should go for a walk," she suggested and watched as Matthew's eyes peered over the top of his newspaper.

"A walk? Where?"

"I don't know. I have a pull to go back up the trail we walked the other day."

"Where you nearly cracked your head open on a rock when you fell to the ground?" he reminded her.

"I can't just sit here," she said as she stood and poured what was left of her coffee into the sink. "I'm going stir crazy."

Matthew folded up the newspaper and sipped at his coffee again. "What do you say we deliver the combination to the safe?"

Grace turned and stared at him. "I have no idea how to approach that. I'm supposed to walk up to the door of this woman's house and say what?"

He tapped his fingers on the table in thought. "Why don't I give it to her? I can say that it was something that was found. Maybe we could put it in an envelope with her name on it and go with that."

"I don't want to lie to people when I'm finalizing someone's wishes."

He nodded in agreement. "If I give it to her, I can tell her that it was given to me, as a reporter, to find the missing person."

"And what? You'll put her on TV?"

He chuckled at that. "Not a bad idea, but no. I'll just do it as a humanitarian gesture."

Grace pressed her fingers to her forehead. "Okay. Let's do it."

AN HOUR after setting down his newspaper, Matthew was sitting in his car outside the house of Evelyn Jackson. The middle-class neighborhood was well groomed and the smell of freshly cut grass filled the air. Matthew thought it was quaint enough to consider for when he and Grace eventually bought a house and raised a family.

He chuckled to himself. They'd moved things fairly quickly, perhaps the thought of marriage and family should be a topic they covered in a few months. Grace had a lot on her plate. He did worry that neither of them had smelled the roses that accompanied his grandmother's nearness. Had she gone away for good when Grace began intercepting the negative spirit?

"Okay, here's the envelope," Grace said snapping him from his thoughts.

He took the envelope she offered and looked down at it. "Well, here we go."

Matthew opened his car door, skirted the front of his car, and walked up the small walk toward the front porch. He was surprised to see the door open and the skeptical face of an older woman in a housecoat peering at him from behind the screen.

"You're that man on TV," she said immediately.

Matthew turned on his newsman smile. "Yes, ma'am. Matthew Campbell from channel four."

The door opened completely now, and he realized this entire moment hinged on the trust he'd built with his viewers.

"What are you doing here?" Mrs. Jackson asked as she pushed open the flimsy screen door that separated them.

"I have something for you," he said as he handed her the envelope, but stood planted on the front porch.

Mrs. Jackson studied it before she tore into it. It was then her eyes went wide. "Where'd you get this?"

"It was delivered to our station. Someone had come across it and wanted our help to find you. Do you know what it is?"

She nodded, her mouth open as if in disbelief at what she held. "Are you a good man, Mr. Campbell?"

"I'd like to think I am, ma'am."

She studied him again. "Come in. Let's see if this is what I think it is."

Matthew looked back at Grace, who waited patiently in the car, and then followed Mrs. Jackson into the house.

She didn't open the windows often, he assumed from the musty smell of food that had been cooked. It wasn't unpleasant, but it said a lot. The shelves of Mrs. Jackson's house were lined with knickknacks of all sorts, and the furniture was draped with quilts. It reminded him somewhat of his grandmother's house. Everything was in its place, but there were a lot of pieces to that everything.

"When my husband died some six years back, he didn't leave me the combination to the safe in our bedroom. He always said he'd provided for us, and he had. But I knew he'd saved and saved, but the bank accounts weren't full. So where was that money?"

"You think it's in the safe?"

"I do."

"Why didn't you have it pried open?"

Mrs. Jackson looked down the hallway as if maybe someone else might walk up on them. "I don't trust my grandkids. I don't want them buying drugs with my money."

"You think your grandkids would do that?"

"That's what all my friends say. I think my grandkids are the cream of the crop, but you know young kids. I don't know what they're really doing." Mrs. Jackson slid the door open on the closet inside her bedroom. "I have a gun in my pocket if you try to steal from me."

"I assure you I would never do that. I should

probably go," Matthew offered, though he seriously doubted the tiny woman had a gun.

"No, I want you to open that safe for me. I can't see those tiny numbers."

Mrs. Jackson was a piece of work, Matthew decided as he knelt down in front of the safe. She trusted him from seeing him on TV and was willing to show him her savings, however, she didn't trust her own grandchildren and thought she could shoot him if he tried to steal from her.

She handed him the piece of paper that he'd concealed in the envelope. With a steady hand, knowing he never was much good with opening his own locker in high school, he began twisting the dial to the numbers that corresponded with the paper.

It took him four tries, but when he heard the click of the lock, he turned to witness a teary-eyed Mrs. Jackson, her hands clutched in front of her as if in prayer.

"Open it. Go on," she said through tears that surfaced in her eyes and in her voice.

Matthew pulled open the door, and he heard the sobbing from behind him. She'd seen the velvet box set in the middle of the safe, propped open with a note that said *Happy Anniversary*.

"Oh, Lord. Give me that," she demanded, and Matthew handed her the box.

She took out one of the large diamond earrings and studied it.

"Damn him. Damn him," she repeated. "I'd asked for these, and he'd never had the means to get me them when our children lived at home. So, I stopped asking."

"It's a very thoughtful gift. How long were you married?"

"Fifty-four years the year he died. We spent our

last anniversary at the hospital. I'd forgotten what day it even was, but he'd had them send up flowers from the gift shop for me. Oh, damn him," she said again as a tear rolled down her cheek. "Is there anything else in there?" she asked, but her eyes were fixed on the earrings.

Matthew leaned into the safe. "There's bundles of money. A few thousand I would assume and some paperwork."

"Yes, damn him again." Now she chuckled. "Those are probably the papers we had to send for to close his estate."

She laughed as she put on one of the earrings and then walked to the mirror over her dresser.

"You've given me a wonderful gift, Mr. Campbell. I'm glad someone sent you that combination. Where did they find it?"

"They didn't say."

"Hmmm." She inspected the earring and then put on the other. "If you ever get the chance to thank that person, please do so. There has been an ache in my heart for years, but today I feel as if he were here with me."

And that was the name of the game, he thought as he stood from his seated position on the floor.

"I should be heading out."

Mrs. Jackson turned to him, the diamond studs sparkling from her ears. "Thank you. There is no way to repay you for this gift."

"My pleasure," he said as he turned and left the house.

Grace sat in the passenger seat looking out the window as he walked toward her. He knew the smile that permeated his lips caught her attention as her lips curled into an equally grand smile.

She didn't say anything until he climbed into the car and they'd pulled away from the curb.

"I can't believe she let you in her house," she said. "I remember her being a very nice woman, but you're a stranger."

"I'm on TV. I have some trust with my viewers," Matthew said in his most news anchor voice and then laughed. "She couldn't read the dial, so she asked me to do it."

"And what was in the safe?"

"Diamond earrings for their anniversary, and some money he'd saved."

Grace sunk into her seat with a sigh. "An anniversary gift? That's precious." She pressed her hands to her chest. "Seriously, that is the sweetest thing."

"She says thank you, by the way. She wanted me to thank whoever had given me that envelope. It made her happy. She said she'd had an ache in her heart for years, but today she felt as though her husband was with her."

Grace bounced in her seat like a child who was excited about a gift. "That's what I want from people. I want them to feel connected."

"You can do that, Grace."

Now she eased back, and her body grew rigid, and her hands were folded tightly in her lap.

"But what about this last one that wants to hurt me? What do they want me to know?"

Matthew reached for her hand and interlaced their fingers. "I don't know, sweetheart, but we're going to find out. What do you say we take a drive? I don't want to get out and walk in this heat, but a drive would be nice."

Grace turned her head so that she looked at him. The tenseness was gone, and the smile replaced. "I'd love that."

"Maybe we'll find somewhere nice to watch the sunset if we're out that long."

She didn't say another word. Instead, Grace let out a low hum of approval.

The truth was, Matthew wanted to drive by the parking lot of the trail they'd walked and see if that car was still there. He hadn't heard from Rebecca again, and now the empty texts had stopped too. He might not love her or want to spend the rest of his life with her, but Rebecca was a friend, and he was growing worried about her.

CHAPTER 35

*M*atthew had driven through a Starbuck's drive-thru on their drive. He'd ordered an iced coffee, while Grace ordered some concoction that was cold and pink.

"You have to taste it. When you order it right it tastes like cereal we used to eat when we were kids," she enthusiastically told him.

"I'm good. That looks like sweetness overload to me."

"You just haven't lived yet," she said as she took a satisfying drink.

He continued to drive with the windows down and the radio playing the oldies station. Grace sang along with the songs, never once commenting on the direction he was driving.

As he turned on the road that would take them just near enough to the parking lot that he could see the cars, his phone began to chime.

"Is this a sign of a breaking news story?" Grace asked as Matthew picked up his phone and saw the numerous texts that scrolled on the screen.

"I'm not sure. I need to pull over."

He noticed that the texts were from Rebecca, and

then there was a string of them from Rebecca's mother.

The texts from Rebecca were the same ones she'd sent days ago after she'd left his house in her fit. Then came a slew of apologies, and yet another handful of angry texts. There were no blank ones now.

He scrolled through them and then opened Rebecca's mother's text.

Have you seen Rebecca? She texted me that she'd been with you and you were in a fight. I haven't seen her in days.

He scrolled to the next text.

Matthew, are you getting my texts? I need your help. I can't find Rebecca, and she hasn't been to her apartment.

Grace rested her hand on his. "Something's wrong."

"Rebecca isn't answering her phone, and her mother is worried."

"You should go. Maybe she's waiting for you to talk to her."

He nodded. "Maybe. Will you be okay at home? Would you like me to take you to your parents' house?"

"I'll be fine. Take me home," she said as he tucked his phone back into his pocket and turned the car back in the other direction.

He slowed as they passed the road toward the trail's parking lot. The car that had looked like Rebecca's was gone. Surely that was a conscience anyway.

MATTHEW DROPPED Grace off at home and headed toward Rebecca's. It seemed to be a silent agreement that having Grace along would have made things worse.

When he got to her apartment, Rebecca's mother was there and raced toward him the moment he pulled up

"They towed her car. She hasn't been home." Her mother gripped the front of his shirt as a means to steer his attention and perhaps keep herself from collapsing to the ground.

Matthew took her hands and guided her to the front step.

"Maggie, slow down and breathe," he said as he inhaled deeply and exhaled to set the example. "There you go."

He let Maggie take a few more breaths, and though he could still feel her shanking, he knew she was slowing her mind and her heart rate.

"Okay, Maggie, where did they find her car?"

"Parking lot. Johnson's trail."

With just the mention of it, Matthew felt his palms grow damp, and his own heart rate picked up.

"What was it doing there?"

"I don't know, Matthew!" she shouted and then buried her face in her hands and sobbed. "I'm sorry. I don't know what to do."

"It's okay. Did she go there often?"

Maggie took a few more deep breaths. "No. I don't think so. I don't know."

"It's okay."

Matthew swallowed down the sickness that was starting to rise in his throat. It had been her car he'd seen on Friday, but had they only just recovered it? And by recovering it, that meant she wasn't with the car.

"Do you think she went for a walk on the trail?" he asked calmly.

"Maybe. She was really mad at you. I'm sorry. Did you know that?" Maggie asked as if it took her thoughts away from the other questions that were brewing and not yet spoken.

"I did. I upset her, but I would never do anything to hurt her," he promised.

"I know." Maggie wiped away a tear. "She wouldn't come to my house for dinner, and the next morning I started to call her, and she wouldn't answer. Well, you know how she gets. I figured she was mad at you so we all would get to suffer."

"She likes to be good and mad," he offered, and he thought he heard the slightest chuckle.

"The police are looking for her."

"Was there a sign of a struggle or anything in her car?"

Maggie shook her head. "No. She parked, and that was it."

"So maybe she did go for a walk or met a friend. I'll get my sources on it, and we'll find her, Maggie."

When Maggie lifted her eyes to him, he saw the fear that shadowed the optimism. "She loves you, Matthew."

"Maybe she'll listen to me then," he said thinking of the many text messages he'd received within just the last hour. "Can I give you a ride home?"

She shook her head. "No. I want to be here when she gets here."

"Will you be okay? Can I send my mother over? My sister?"

Again, she shook her head. "I'll be fine. Thank you."

As he drove away, he didn't feel as if he could offer Maggie Barnes any comfort. There was a nagging tug in his chest that told him he should have gone closer to the car when he'd seen it. He'd been sure it was hers, and now he wondered if she was trailing him and Grace.

Parts of him wanted to be angry if she'd gone that far. His life was his life, and there was no room for Rebecca Barnes in it. But never, ever, had he wanted harm to come to her. Even if she'd followed them up the trail, wouldn't she have come back? They were back within the hour.

Then, the thought crossed his mind. Grace had had to leave the trail when she'd fainted and was nearly choking on the dirt.

Was this more than a spirit trying to harm Grace? Was this a spirit trying to tell her something? Were they trying to lead her to Rebecca who needed her help?

Now the sickness made him dizzy as he navigated the streets speeding toward Grace's house.

Pulling up on the curb, he slammed the car into park and ran for the front door. Pushing it open, he could smell the thick scent of newly turned earth.

"Grace?" he stood in the entry for a moment and then slowly made his way through the house. "Grace, where are you?"

He heard the faint sound of pounding coming from down the hall, then he realized he could hear water.

Matthew hurried down the hall nearly sliding on the water the pooled under the bathroom door and into the hallway.

"Grace!" He tried to push open the door only to find it was locked. "Open the door, Grace. Open the door!"

Again, he pushed against it without any movement. Then he smelled the slightest fragrance of roses, and the lock on the door clicked.

Matthew pushed it open to see Grace flailing in the water. He rushed to her, pulling her to the surface and against him.

"Grace! Stay with me, Grace."

She gasped for air and coughed as she gasped some more. "Held me. They held me."

"Who held you?"

"They held me down. Couldn't breathe."

The scratch on her neck was fresh again. Matthew pulled her from the tub and fell to the floor with her on his lap. Pulling the towel from the rod, he wrapped it around them as she shook against him.

"It attacked you again, didn't it?"

She nodded as she tried to catch her breath. "Dirt. I smell dirt."

The longer he sat on the cold, wet floor with Grace pressed against him, the more he worried that the two incidences were related. How was it that Grace was attacked the same day that Rebecca disappeared?

No, that didn't make sense. He was still receiving texts from Rebecca. Again, one didn't have anything to do with the other.

"I smelled roses before the door opened," he said with his lips pressed to the top of Grace's wet hair. "I think my grandmother let me in."

"Good," she managed, her teeth audibly chattering. "Someone is trying to kill me."

"Shhh," he whispered in her ear as he rocked her like a child. "I think someone is just trying to tell you something. We're going to figure this out, Grace. You and I are going to see this through and figure it out."

$\mathcal{O}$nce Grace had calmed, Matthew helped her dress. Now bundled in a comfy pair of sweat pants, under a fuzzy blanket, she sipped on a warm cup of tea, while he sat in the blistering heat on the back porch trying to sort through his laptop for connections that might be able to do some searches on Rebecca.

He first had called her mother, who still hadn't heard from her. He checked in with Pamela and found out that there had been nothing come through on the wire that said they'd lost or found a woman, and a car parked in a lot could have just been stolen. Matthew's connection at the fire department and the police station had come up with nothing.

Rebecca Barnes had vanished in thin air. As he looked at his phone, he thought of the blank texts that had appeared on his other phone before it exploded in his hand. What was that about? Had that been a malfunction in the phone, or had that been something else entirely? Was this too a sign from beyond? And if it was, why were they working through Rebecca?

Then, as if the weather had gone from the heat of

summer to the depths of winter, the air around him froze, and his breath carried on the stilled air.

His muscles shook from the cold, but as he sat in the chair, still seeing the blooming roses from beyond the grayness that surrounded him, he feared the worst.

Matthew willed away the chill, and when he could, he ran back into the house to Grace.

GRACE WAS FINALLY WARMING UP, but she swore she'd never—ever—take another bath. And, if the dead were going to continue to try and kill her, she was going to find a new job and stop helping them. She'd had enough of the pushing, the cold, the scratching, the smell, and of course the attempted drowning. Seriously, there had to be a better way to get her attention.

She lifted her mug to her lips just as she heard the backdoor slam and Matthew ran into the room, his face bright red and his breath labored.

Grace sat up, putting her feet on the floor, and her mug on the coffee table.

"What happened to you? Did you get attacked too?"

Matthew shook his head. "No. Something happened, but I wasn't attacked. But I think I know what's going on."

"Please, fill me in."

"No one is trying to kill you. I think they're trying to get your attention."

"They have it."

He moved to her now and took her hand. Grace flinched when she felt the ice cold of his skin.

"What happened outside?"

"I was looking for some leads, and when I came up with the idea, the air froze. I could see my breath."

"Death was surrounding you."

"Something like that."

"What idea did you have?"

He turned to face her. His eyes bore the sadness of whatever he was taking so long to form the words about.

"I think it's Rebecca, and I think something bad has happened to her."

Grace realized her breathing had stopped for a moment as she took in what he was telling her.

"You think she's the one doing this? She's trying to get our attention?"

He nodded. "She wants us to find her."

"And these are all clues to something bigger?"

His hands gripped hers tighter now. "Grace, I think she's dead."

Grace eased back against the couch and thought about what he was saying. If it was Rebecca, and she was trying to get their attention, was she showing them what happened to her through the attacks on Grace? The shove, the scratch, the dirt? The dirt!

"She's on the trail," Grace spat out the words and stood, kicking the blanket off from around her legs.

"How do you know that?"

"That's where I smelled the dirt more clearly. That's where I was when I lost consciousness, and that's where her car was."

A MIX of guilt and the vile taste of regret stirred in Matthew's belly. If she'd followed them onto the trail, had she gotten hurt then? Why hadn't he stopped and checked if it was her car? Then again, Grace had been attacked before that. Was it only fate that they'd gone hiking on that trail? Had Rebecca already been there?

The thought that they might find her and that something had happened paralyzed him on that couch as Grace ran through the house changing her clothes and gathering items in a backpack.

What if they were right? What if Rebecca Barnes were dead? That guilt began to gather weight, and he could feel it pull him down. Somehow, he needed to push it away. He wasn't responsible for anything that might have happened to Rebecca. He didn't love her, and that was it. He hadn't been mean or abusive. Any actions she took after she left his house were hers.

"Let's go," Grace said standing in the doorway now dressed in a pair of jeans, a large brimmed hat on her head, and fully prepared backpack on her shoulder. "It's going to be dark in four hours. That's all the time we have."

All the time we have, he heard her words replay in his head as he walked to his car. They had less than four hours to find Rebecca Barnes on the Jackson Trail, dead or alive.

* * *

BEFORE THEY MADE it to the trail, Matthew put in a call to Kyle. He was a trained medic who had served multiple tours in Afghanistan.

He would know what to expect if they found her. If she were alive, how would they help her? If she were dead, how they handle it? And, the looming question would be, what would happen to Grace on the trail?

Kyle pulled into the lot a moment after Matthew parked car. He jumped from his truck, grabbed a backpack from the bed of his truck, and flung it on his back.

"Did you call the authorities?" Kyle asked.

Matthew climbed from the car and slid his sunglasses to the top of his head. "No. It's just the three of us."

Kyle shifted his jaw and inched in closer. "You think some woman might be dead up there, and you didn't call?"

"It's more complicated than that," Matthew said flatly. "If you're uncomfortable, you don't have to be here." Matthew locked the car key fob, saw Grace come around the back of the car.

"No need to get worked up," Kyle said. "You have never steered me wrong. Who are we looking?"

Grace moved in next to Kyle. "We have reason to believe that Rebecca Barnes might have been following us the other day and has since gone missing. Her car was towed from the parking lot."

Kyle nodded slowly. "So maybe she fell, and no one saw her?"

"Yes," Matthew agreed. "Something like that."

"Let's get going then. You're running out of daylight."

Matthew watched as Kyle started up the trail, a man on a mission to find a woman he didn't know.

Exchanging glances with Grace, he moved to her. "Are you feeling okay?"

"I can smell dirt, I feel like I swallowed a gallon of water through my nose, and there is a faint scent of roses. So, I think your grandmother is here to help."

"I don't want you to do this if you think it will hurt you," he said resting his hand on her cheek.

"If it's her trying to get through to us, then we owe her this."

Gently, he pressed his lips to hers. "I love you. If you, at any time, want to turn back..."

"I will let you know. Now, stop stalling," she said. "We're running out of daylight, and I can't stand the smell of dirt anymore."

CHAPTER 37

*D*irt clogged Grace's nose and throat. Her eyes burned and her vision blurred, but she wasn't going to tell Matthew about it. She was going to keep hiking up that trail until they found something.

Kyle was at least a quarter of a mile ahead of them. Matthew continued to turn back and look at her, but Grace smiled and kept walking.

She'd already downed a bottle of water trying to clear her throat, but nothing was helping.

Another fifteen minutes and they were at the spot where she'd fallen when they'd taken their walk.

Kyle stood with them now, a bottle of water being chugged down, and sweat lining the neck of his shirt.

"This is as far as you got last time?" he asked, and Matthew nodded as he collected his breath while sitting on a boulder.

"Yeah, we ate lunch here," Matthew offered as he exchanged glances with Grace, but said nothing about her passing out there.

Kyle lifted his head and looked around. "There's another path that starts just ahead and goes back south a bit. If memory serves correctly, there is a small creek or something about a mile down the path."

"A creek? Is it very deep?" Grace asked trying to clear the dirt from her throat and not let on that the water was some kind of key to this mystery.

"Yeah, I suppose it could get deep. It's not some raging river, but enough to lounge in if you were hot."

Or drown in if someone held you under, Grace thought to herself as she could now smell the water.

"I think we should go that way," she suggested as she hiked her backpack up onto her back again after tucking her bottle of water in the pocket.

"Let's go," Kyle said as he looked at his watch and then headed down the trail.

Matthew waited for her at the head to the new trail. "You're sure? You don't look so well."

"I'm fine. Let's just keep going. I can smell dirt and taste it. And now the water—we have to keep going."

"If at any time you…"

"I know. If I have to stop or have an episode, I'll let you know. But someone is still trying to lead us on, and we owe it to them to try and figure out what they want."

"You think it's Rebecca?"

Grace shrugged. "I don't know. But we need to find out."

But she was sure they both knew it was Rebecca who was leading them down the trail, and Grace was sure their time had already run out.

MATTHEW HEARD the water long before he could see it beyond the trees. A need burst through him as if he should run, but he refrained. Kyle was a reasonable distance in front of them, and he'd let them know if he found anything. But even though Matthew wanted answers, he prayed that Kyle kept walking.

Grace was coughing now, which meant the dirt she could smell, and taste was causing her problems. He'd have liked her to have stayed home or in the car, but she was their compass. Without Grace, he and Kyle would be lost.

He'd slowed his pace to wait for Grace, who seemed to slow as they'd gotten closer to the creek that Kyle had told them about. He wondered just how much this was physically challenging her. As he stopped to wait for her, he heard Kyle yell for him.

"She's here! She's here! I found her!"

Matthew wanted to run, but his legs had suddenly turned to pudding, and he froze in place until Grace ran to him.

"Oh, God. He found her?" she gasped.

Nothing came from his throat when he tried to use his voice. Kyle was with Rebecca, and Matthew didn't want to move.

Grace had continued past him, still coughing, but now almost running toward Kyle.

He needed to break from the paralysis and move. What would happen to Grace if Rebecca were dead? Would Rebecca hurt her? Would something happen to Grace?

Forcing himself from where he'd stopped, he hurried toward them, his heart slamming in his chest and his breath stuck in his lungs.

When he reached them, just beyond the trees, Kyle's hands were on Grace's arms, and he was shaking her.

"What's going on?" Matthew hurried to them.

"She's having some kind of seizure or something," Kyle said as he tried to ease himself to the ground with Grace. "She looked at her and then this." He laid her on the ground and rolled to the side of her.

Matthew fell to her side. "Grace. Grace, what is it?"

When her eyes opened, he knew she wasn't there with them. Whoever was looking up at him wasn't Grace. It wasn't until her wide eyes locked on his, and the corner of her mouth turned up into a sly little grin did he understand.

"Rebecca?"

"You took too long, Matthew. You took too long," her voice rose, but now it had sass to it. "You're too late."

Grace's eyes closed and she began to cough again, but now she expelled water. Matthew turned her to her side as she threw up water, just as she might have if she'd been in the creek face down.

It wasn't until Grace had eased back against him that he turned his head to see Rebecca's arm flung over a rock, the rest of her body submerged in the creek.

"She's been there for a few days," Kyle said. "We don't want to move her until the authorities get here."

Matthew wrapped his arms around Grace and held on to her tightly. *Authorities.* They would only need the authorities to arrive if she were dead, and that was what Kyle was telling them.

He looked down at Grace, whose eyes had softened. "Are you okay?"

"Yeah," she said, her voice raspy. "I'm okay."

Kyle watched them both. "And what was it that happened to you?"

How were they going to explain that, Matthew wondered?

Grace laughed. "Let's say that this heat is getting the better of me. I need to get back to the car."

"I can wait for the police," Kyle offered.

"Thank you." Grace closed her eyes and rested in Matthew's arms.

When she was ready to walk again, they started back down the trail.

Just as they'd reached the car, the police, with sirens blaring, turned into the lot. They blocked the entrance, stopping their exit.

Matthew let go of Grace and walked toward the officer that came toward him.

"My associate Kyle Patterson is up on the southern fork of Johnson's trail about a quarter of the mile down by the creek. He's with a body that was found which we believe to be Miss Rebecca Barnes."

The officer wrote down the information as Matthew gave it to him.

"You know Miss Barnes?"

"I do," he said and swallowed hard as he thought of Grace looking up at him and repeating Rebecca's words. "I spoke to her mother this morning, and she told me they had recovered her car from this lot. We headed up the trail to look for her."

"We had officers in the area yesterday, but they didn't find anything."

Matthew bit down on his lip to keep it from trembling. "I assumed she'd followed us up here the other day, though we hadn't met up on the trail. She seems to have veered off from where we were."

"We need you to stay here," the officer motioned to another officer who gave him a nod. "We'll let you know when you're free to leave."

Matthew moved back to the car where Grace waited for him. "What did they say?"

"We have to wait here."

"That's fine," she acknowledged the officer who watched them. "They're headed up to her, right?"

"Yeah. I can't tell if they're suspicious of me, or it's just their nature."

Grace placed her hand on his cheek. "They have to work the scene. We found her. They have to assume we could have left her there to begin with. We had nothing to do with his, Matthew."

He wasn't so sure about that, and it ate at him even as he looked into the loving eyes of this woman he loved. No, he physically hadn't harmed her, but he'd broken her heart and driven her to follow him —to die.

Matthew rubbed his hand over the back of his neck. "Let's get you in the car and turn on the air. You're flushed."

"Feeling as if you're drowning takes a lot out of a person. It was like the bathtub all over again."

As he opened the door for her, he looked at her. "Is that all you remember?"

"Yeah. I got to Kyle and water filled my throat and my nose. I couldn't breathe. Then, when I came to, I was coughing it all up, and you were holding me."

Trying to keep his composure he simply nodded. "But you're okay, right?"

"I'll be fine. I'm going to close my eyes for a moment."

"That's a good idea."

Matthew handed her the keys and closed the door to the car as she started the engine.

He walked toward the back of the car and rested against it with his face buried in his hands.

Grace didn't remember having Rebecca come through her to scold him. Had that happened before?

This had become a much deeper problem than just Grace hearing people give her last requests. What had his grandmother gotten her into?

Sickness stirred inside of him. Rebecca blamed

him, even in death she held a grudge. What if she continued to hurt Grace? What if others did the same thing? And what if this was all his fault? It was, after all, his grandmother that opened her up to this.

Matthew lifted his head as he watched Kyle decent the hill and walk toward him.

"They're processing the scene. We're all going to have to head to the police station and give statements."

"Right. Yeah, that makes sense." Matthew raked his fingers through his hair.

Kyle rested his hand on Matthew's shoulder. "Are you okay, man? You look sick."

"It's a lot to take in. I didn't really think we'd find her—not like that."

"There's a lot to go through. They'll figure out what happened to her."

"You don't think someone did that? I mean, someone didn't kill her?"

Kyle turned his head and looked back toward the trail. "How close to her were you?"

"Friends. We've been friends since high school. Nothing really close," he said and then realized that it hadn't even been two weeks since she slept next to him in his bed.

"I don't want to upset you."

"You know me," Matthew said urging Kyle. "Tell me what you think."

"I think she tried to commit suicide, but it didn't quite work out the way she'd planned, and she ended up drowning instead."

"Suicide?"

"Yeah. Her wrists were cut, but not to where she would have bled out right away. It looked more like a way to get some attention." And that, he thought, would be exactly like Rebecca. "There's a cut on her neck too, but that might have been from when she fell into the creek."

Matthew ran his hand over his hair. She'd killed herself—over him? It was hard to wrap his head around.

Kyle gave Matthew's shoulder a squeeze. "It'll all be okay. Is Grace okay? I've never quite seen a seizure like that or heat stroke. It was completely different, and I've seen everything."

"She'll be fine."

Kyle nodded and turned to talk to the officer who had been stationed to keep an eye on the entrance to the lot.

Matthew took in a few deep breaths. The sickness that had moved through him now sat like a weight in his stomach, and it tightened with the pang of guilt. Rebecca Barnes had tried to commit suicide, and he had to assume it was because he didn't love her.

CHAPTER 38

They'd kept them in the lot until they were ready to bring Rebecca down and put her in the van that had arrived.

Kyle met Matthew and Grace at the police station, where they all gave statements, individually, and were released.

Matthew took Grace, under protest, to her parents' house, and he headed to Maggie Barnes' house.

The woman on the sofa was just a shell of the woman he'd talked to earlier that day. She'd been presented with the news of her daughter's death, and her eyes were sunken and hollow.

A cousin, one Matthew had met years earlier, had met him at the door and escorted him into Maggie. He could hear the rustling in the kitchen which told him that family had arrived the moment they'd that Rebecca was missing.

Maggie looked up at him, but as if she were too weak to rise, she held out her hand for him to take as he sat next to her.

"Maggie, I'm so sorry," he said as she rested her head on his shoulder. "I wish I had words."

"She's gone, Matt. She's gone," Maggie sobbed, and he held her.

"I know. I know."

"Suicide. They said it was suicide, but I don't know. I just can't imagine she was that sad. Rebecca was never sad."

As he held onto Maggie, he thought about that very statement. He'd have to argue that perhaps that was why Rebecca was the way she was. She was sad, all the time. Not on the surface, but deep inside he knew she wasn't happy.

She flitted around and fussed over everything, but he'd been around Rebecca enough to know she never felt as though things went her way. And, wasn't he proof of that? She wanted him, and he'd let her down. He had a slew of hateful texts to prove it.

That ball of guilt grew more substantial in his gut. It was much too late to change his mind now—for her sake. He hadn't loved her, but he'd never have wished death on her either.

"Tell me how I can help you. I'm at your service, Maggie."

Rebecca's mother looked up at him. "She loved you, Matt. I know it sounds stupid, but she did. She talked about you all the time."

He swallowed hard. "I didn't know that," he lied.

"She was devastated when your grandmother died. She knew it was going to tear you apart."

"She was there for me," he admitted, even if he'd done everything he could to turn her away.

"They'll do an autopsy on her. Doesn't that sound awful."

"They'll respect her."

Maggie nodded. "I sent her cousin over to her house to look for a note or something. I'm lost, Matt. So lost."

"Maybe you should rest. Can I escort you to your room?"

Maggie nodded again. "I think that would be nice." They stood, and he balanced her as he walked her down the hallway. "I'd like to have that mortuary do her funeral. The one that did your grandmother's."

Matthew forced a smile to his lips. "Of course. They did a wonderful job for us. I can talk to them if you'd like."

Maggie let out a grateful sigh and looked up at him again, this time with only tired eyes that appreciated him. "Thank you. That would help."

"You rest. I'll call and make some preliminary arrangements and come back by later."

She gave him a smile before walking into the room and closing the door.

* * *

Grace had been asleep on her mother's sofa since Matthew had dropped her off. Only the smell of spaghetti sauce simmering on the stove had awakened her.

The sun had started to set, which meant it was much later than she'd initially thought.

Sitting up, and resting her feet on the floor, she realized she no longer could smell dirt. She assumed that message had been received loud and clear—it had only taken them days to decipher it though.

Guilt sickened her. If she'd had known what it was that day on the trail, would they have found her? Would they have found her in time?

From the kitchen she heard her mother and father talking, and then she heard Matthew's voice.

How had she slept through him arriving?

Slowly, she rose from the sofa and walked toward the kitchen at the back of the house. Her parents sat at the table with Matthew. He and her father each nursed a beer, while her mother had wine.

"You look like you feel better," her mother said when she noticed her standing in the doorway.

"I guess I was exhausted. What time is it?"

"Almost nine o'clock. We were holding dinner for you."

"You didn't have to do that," Grace said as she walked toward Matthew who held out his hand to her. "How is her family?" she asked him before sitting on his knee.

"Heartbroken. Her mother is a bit out of sorts, but the house is filled with family. Her mother would like your family to take care of the services. I told her I would talk to you."

Her mother sipped her wine. "I told him we would take good care of her."

Grace took Matthew's beer and took a long pull from it. "Do you think that's a good idea? I mean the woman tried to kill me."

"I think she needed help. I don't think she intended to kill you," her mother offered, though her voice didn't resonate with assurance. "Besides, we think it's best if we take care of everything, and you don't return to work until after her services. It would just be safer that way."

"I feel like a burden on everyone."

Matthew patted her knee. "You're not a burden. Remember this is a unique gift, and now we know it has more to it."

"More to it? She tried to drown me in my bathtub," Grace said and realized they hadn't shared that with her parents yet. "But, Matthew got home in time."

Her father shook his head. "I never would have let you…"

"What? Never let me be part of the family business if you knew this would happen? None of us knew. And fine, if Rebecca Barnes needs a farewell message sent on too, then she'll get one. I know now what was happening. I'll pay more attention."

Her mother let out a groan into her wine glass, and Grace realized she didn't believe her own words either, but they were out. She'd agreed to pass on last goodbyes, and damnit, she was going to do just that.

WHEN THE DINNER plates had been cleaned away, and her parents had gone to bed, Grace sat with Matthew on the back porch and listened to the crickets chirp.

"I brought a bag of your things over. I want you to stay here with your parents tonight," he said as he brushed his thumb over her knuckles.

"I'm an adult. I can handle myself."

"And Rebecca tried to kill you from her watery grave, I'm not chancing it."

"Fine, and where will you be?"

"I'm going home for the night and arranging my things. I think I'd better print out all those text messages she sent me and turn them over to the police. Maybe my broken phone too. And," he took a breath, "tomorrow I'm going to her mother's and helping her family make arrangements."

Grace tightened her jaw. There was no reason to be bitter or jaded over his wanting the help the family of his friend, but she couldn't help but feel as if a knife had been sunk into her back.

"So she was that important to you? You're going to take time off from work to manage her affairs?"

"Grace, they need some help. I can offer that."

"For her?"

"For them." He turned to look at her, but she shifted her eyes from him. "Look at me."

Grace turned and did as he asked, but by his reaction, she knew that the anger she felt during inside of her reached her eyes.

"No matter what Rebecca wanted from me, I didn't want the same thing. You know that. I made my decision very clear."

"And now here you are…"

"Helping the family of a friend. Don't read into this. What does it help? She's dead, Grace. Dead."

The sassy child in her wanted to correct him —*deceased*—but she refrained and let him continue.

"You have your calling, and I have mine. Together they'll work out just fine if you don't think that I'm betraying you each time I try to help someone out."

Grace took a breath to argue but realized he was right. That was precisely what she felt.

"I'll be back tomorrow," he said as he stood. "I'll be in touch with your mother tomorrow too to finalize Rebecca's arrangements for when they release her."

"Fine." She'd wanted to stand and kiss him good-bye, but she couldn't bring herself to do it.

"I'll talk to you tomorrow then." With that, he turned and went back into the house.

A moment later she heard his car start and drive away, leaving her alone with her jilted thoughts on the back porch.

As she sat there, she realized the crickets had gone quiet, but the scent of roses filled the air.

"You might as well scold me too," she said to the air as it stirred around her. "I'm being an ass, but I can't help it. I love him, and it hurts."

The warmth of the night wrapped around her like a hug and she eased back in her seat.

"I think there is more that Rebecca wants to say, but I'm afraid of her. I didn't know someone could interrupt me being me, and she did that."

The air shifted again, and she heard a faint voice whisper in her ear.

I'll always protect you.

CHAPTER 39

$\mathcal{M}$atthew didn't call or text Grace at all. Her mother had mentioned that he'd been in to see her, but he hadn't reached out to her with an apology—or to ask for one.

Grace was going stir crazy in her parents' house. No one wanted her to be anywhere else, and that was driving her mad.

The man she loved was spending time with the family of a woman who had caused Grace pain—physically and emotionally. Why was it that even in her absence Grace was still angry?

It didn't help that the scent of roses followed her into each room she walked into. Perhaps it was as if Nora Campbell was taking care of her, but even that was beginning to piss her off. All she wanted to do was get back to work as usual. If it would make things better, she'd even go buy a brand-new pair of noise-canceling earphones so that she couldn't hear a thing.

It went deeper than just ignoring them now, she considered as she pressed the button on the instant coffee maker to make yet another cup of liquid energy.

If a spirit wanted to get to her, they could even bypass Nora from the other side and reach her. They could hurt her. They could even kill her.

She shook her head as the machine spat amber gold into her cup. Rebecca was showing her what she'd been going through. The scratch on her neck was to mimic her own. Perhaps the dirt was where she'd fallen, and maybe—just maybe, she hadn't died when she'd first come for Grace. Was she reaching out as she slipped away? But the creek and the bathtub, that was different. Grace could have drowned—just as Rebecca had. Was she leading Grace to her or trying to share her fate?

Picking up the cup, Grace poured it down the drain in the sink and left the mug for later. She had to do something, and the only thing she could think of was to go to the cemetery and at least sit with Nora. If that went well, then she'd go to the mortuary. If it didn't go well, at least there would be people nearby to help her.

Determined to pick up her life again, Grace headed out leaving her phone on the counter so that no one could call her to change her mind.

* * *

GRACE NOTICED THAT HER MOTHER, father, and brother were all at work. Their cars were parked in the back lot with the other employees. There were two different hearses parked on either side of the building, meaning multiple funerals were going on. They needed her, she thought as she continued driving through the cemetery.

Usually, funerals were scattered throughout the week, but once in a while, it happened that they had to multi-task onsite. It was an all-hands-on-deck situation, only she was being excluded.

As she turned the last corner toward Nora's gravesite, she batted her eyes against the tears that were forming. How stupid was she to be having a pity party over not being at work and not being part of funerals for people she didn't know? It was sick. She should be committed.

That thought had her laughing through the tears, and the smell of roses filled the car.

"I'm being stupid. I know that," she said as if Nora were right there with her.

Grace parked the car behind another car on the narrow lane. When she looked out to spot the other person, she realized it was Matthew's mother standing over Nora's grave with a bouquet of flowers in her hand.

Would she even notice if Grace drove off? But then Angela Campbell raised her hand in a wave.

Grace waved back as she turned off the engine and stepped out of her car.

Remembering to keep a smile on her face, she walked to Angela who moved to hug her when she approached her.

"The rosebush we planted at the house that was Nora's has exploded with buds. I was sure she'd like to have some," Angela offered as she looked down at the flowers in her hand. "I added a few flowers from my garden as well."

"They're lovely."

Angela set them on the ground next to the temporary marker. "I also came to see you, but they said you were out sick." She lifted her eyes and scanned them over Grace. "You look as if you're feeling better."

"I've had a few hard days, that's all. It's not an easy job."

"Oh, dear, I can't even imagine what you do every day. And then for you and Matthew to have come across Rebecca like you did..." Angela wiped a tear from her eye. "That was horrible."

When Angela reached for Grace's hand, her first instinct was to pull away, but somehow it eased Grace.

"Matthew is finding comfort in helping her family," Grace said, hoping that her voice carried with it some sincerity.

"He's got a kind and gentle soul. I think that's why you found each other. You have a kind and gentle soul too."

In the past few days, Grace had come to wonder if that was true. If death had been such a part of her life, and she'd never had a problem with it, why did Matthew's role in it cause her concern?

"You said you came to see me?" Grace asked, realizing that Angela had mentioned it.

"I did. I have something for you." Reaching into her purse, Angel pulled out a small white box with a red ribbon tied around it. "My husband and I would like you to have this."

Grace's hand shook as she accepted the box and pulled the ribbon from it. The moment she lifted the lid, tears pooled in her eyes.

Pulling out the bumblebee pin, she let the tears spill down her cheeks. "Oh, Angela. I can't take this."

"Oh, yes you can," she said as she laughed. "You understand it. The fact that you bought one and wore it to her funeral—" She clasped her hands over her heard. "We knew Nora would have adored you, and Matthew sure does."

"Shouldn't this go to your daughter?"

Angela placed her hand over Grace's, securing the pin between them. "Brittany has a million little things that her grandmother gave her over the years. She thought it belonged with you as well, and Nora had left it for Matthew. With her wedding veil," she said on a laugh. "He wore the pin one day and then gave it back to us. He didn't feel as though it belonged to him or was his decision to give it to someone."

When Angela pulled back her hand, Grace looked down at the pin. Drawing it from the box, she studied it. The scent of roses blew through the cemetery and Angela took in a deep breath.

"Oh, my. Are there rose bushes nearby? That was quite a wind."

"I think that came from the roses you brought. They are very fragrant."

"They are. My car smells delightful. May I pin it on you?" Angela took the pin from Grace and held it up.

With a simple nod, Grace agreed knowing Nora was there with them and pleased.

Angela pinned the bumblebee to Grace's shirt and then took a step back to admire it. "I know she'd love that," she said clasping her hands together. "I'm delighted that you took such good care of her, and that you found Matthew as well. It's almost as if Nora arranged it all herself."

Grace laughed at that but wondered if Angela had any idea how Nora had arranged it all.

"I should be going. I made a casserole for the Barnes family, and I want to take it by. Would you and Matthew like to come by for dinner? We'd love to have you."

Grace took a breath to answer and then remembered she'd left her phone at her parents' house. "Can

I get back to you? I haven't talked to him today, and I left my phone at home."

"Of course. You let me know." She leaned in a pressed a kiss to Grace's cheek. "I'll talk to you soon."

Grace watched as Angela walked toward her car and waved as she drove away.

Looking down at the bouquet that rested next to Nora's name, she laughed. "Are you sure you want me to have this pin? I'm not sure your grandson is thrilled with me right now."

Instead of the scent of roses filling the air, Grace heard her name shouted from another section in the cemetery. When she looked up, she saw Mr. Rodriguez pulling chairs from the back of his car, and next to him was Mrs. Fallon, who waved as well.

Grace returned the wave and laughed. "I just need to see what Rebecca has to say, then I can move on with more goodbyes."

Go on. The voice was but a whisper in her ear.

CHAPTER 40

As she passed Mr. Rodriguez, Mrs. Fallon, and Mr. Leeds Grace only waved. Something was pulling her to the mortuary now.

The parking lot was full of cars. Her parents and her brother would be monitoring one service, while there was probably a visitation behind handled by Chase and Ella.

She would park in the back, among the others, and slip through the side door. There was something pulling her toward the building now, and she hoped it wouldn't hurt her.

Parking her car next to her brother's, Grace climbed out, brushed the wrinkles from her pants, and started for the door. She could hear the music from the chapel and knew that the funeral was in progress. Perhaps she could make it out of the building before anyone saw her.

Holding the door so it wouldn't make any noise, Grace let it close and turned around to find herself face to face with Matthew.

She gasped and stumbled back a step. "I didn't expect you to be here. What are you doing here?"

He rose a brow. "Perhaps I should ask you the same thing. I thought you were waiting this out."

Letting her shoulders drop, she moved to him. "I can't. I think she has more to say. Is she here?"

Matthew pressed his lips together. "Yes. Ella let me know they had received her."

Grace drew in a deep breath and found comfort that it was filled with his cologne. "She won't be presentable, but do you want to see her?"

"What I want is you to go home. I don't want anything to happen to you." He reached for her now and took her hands in his. "I love you, and frankly all of this scares the crap out of me. I'm tired, emotional, and scared. That doesn't make me a very good partner."

"Then don't send me away. Let me be with you when you're at your most vulnerable," she said as she gave his hands a squeeze. "I have it under good authority that I'll be protected."

A smile came to his lips. "My grandmother?"

Grace tapped the pin on her blouse. "Yes."

His eyes opened wide. "That's not your pin. That's my grandmother's pin."

"You can tell that?"

"Yes. It's a custom piece. Yours is close, but..." He reached up and touched it. "How did you get this?"

"Your mother gave it to me. She said even your sister thought I should have it."

His smile grew wider. "That's a sign, isn't it?"

"Is it?"

Matthew nodded resting his palm against her cheek. "It's been a crazy few weeks, hasn't it? When my grandmother got sick, I can tell you that finding the woman of my dreams was not the first thing I was thinking of. But then I saw you..."

Grace sighed. "And I never thought that this job

would put me in the path to find someone. I was sure that was what was holding me back."

He chuckled. "It was just saving you for me." Matthew turned his head and looked down the hallway. "Are you sure you want to talk to her? This is when you're most open."

"I think she has more to say. And if you go with me then..."

"Then I can protect you."

"I think she was trying to get my attention and not purposefully trying to kill me."

He chuckled again. "She got your attention alright, but I'm not so sure trying to get your attention in the bathtub was the right tactic."

Grace took his hand, interlacing their fingers, and began to walk to the back of the building where they kept those who had just arrived.

In all of the times Matthew had gone behind the scenes for a story, he'd never been taken into a cold room where they kept the dead—especially with the thought he'd be communicating with them.

The room wasn't unlike what he'd had in mind. It was cold, and there was a wall of doors, much like he'd seen on NCIS a thousand times.

Grace checked a chart that hung on the wall before walking to one of the doors.

"Are you sure you want to be here?" She looked up at Matthew, her eyes filled with concern for his well-being. Wasn't that funny? He was sure he was there to protect her.

"I saw her, remember."

Grace shook her head. "It'll be different."

"I'm okay." He steadied himself anyway.

She kept her eyes on him for a moment longer before pulling open the little door.

He saw the top of her head. Her blonde hair was dull and matted. The thought that this was what Grace had to deal with daily made him nauseous.

Matthew watched as Grace gently pulled out the drawer where Rebecca lay, pale, marred, and dead.

He found himself needing to remind himself to breathe and thought he might need a chair.

Grace let out a slow breath as he sucked in another. "She's calmed down a bit," Grace said.

"What did she say?"

"She's upset that you're seeing her like this, and she thinks you should leave."

Matthew shook his head. "No. I'm fine. I want to know what she has to say."

Grace stood looking down at Rebecca shaking her head and then nodding. She touched the pin on her shirt and batted her eyes as if she wanted to cry.

"Well? What is she saying?"

Grace held up a finger signaling him to be patient, but he found he had no patience left when it came to Rebecca Barnes, even in death.

"She loves you," Grace said, her voice cracking under the words. "She hates me for taking you away from her."

"You didn't take me away from her. I didn't…" She held up her hand again to stop him from speaking— to prevent him from upsetting a dead woman.

"She hadn't meant to die. All she wanted was some attention in a moment of need."

Need? More like a moment of self-pity.

Grace nodded again. "When she attacked me in the room, she was just trying to get my attention."

"She did that to you? She admitted it?"

"Yes. She was slipping between life and death and

was scared. She managed through your grandmother and attacked me."

"What about the phone calls and texts?"

Grace listened again. "She was mad. She doesn't know how she did it, but she exploded your phone wanting to hurt you. But," she quickly added, "she's glad it didn't hurt you."

The sickness that swarmed in his belly began to aside as the anger grew. He looked down at Rebecca, who lay cold and still before him. "You wanted to hurt me for not giving into you? You hurt Grace. You nearly killed her. For what?"

Grace reached for him, over the top of Rebecca, but just as she touched him she stood erect, shoulders back, and the expression on her face was one he'd seen a million times.

"I wanted to marry you. I deserved your love, and you never gave it to me. You let me sleep in your bed, you kissed me, and yet you were callous and mean." The words were Rebecca's even if they came through Grace—he'd seen the transformation take place right before him, or he'd never had believed it.

"I wasn't mean," he said looking into Grace's eyes, but well aware he was having his last argument with Rebecca. "I appreciated the company. I couldn't have told you that I'd meet Grace and fall in love. You can't dictate that."

"She's new to you."

"And you're dead," he reminded her with words so calculated they hurt to say.

As if she'd forgotten, Grace looked down at the body of the spirit that now spoke to Matthew. "She's kind. Kind to the point it almost burns."

He couldn't help but smile. He knew that, but to have someone tell him that about Grace from the inside, well that justified everything he'd been contemplating.

"Rebecca, she can help you. It's too late for you or us in this realm. You made that decision."

"I didn't want to die."

"Then why did you do what you did?"

Grace bit down on her lip. "I wanted your attention. I wanted you to care that something bad happened to me. But I slipped into the creek, and I couldn't get back out."

"You led us up there. I haven't been there in years."

"We were there together once."

He thought about it and then remembered they had hiked there after her first divorce. He'd kissed her to calm her, and that had been all. How demented was she to have carried something so simple with her for all those years?

"That was a long time ago."

"I wanted you to remember it. But I went too far. Once I committed, I couldn't get off the trail."

"You were dying right away, Grace felt it."

"But you didn't come for me. Neither of you came for me. You were only feet away, and you left."

He thought about watching Grace that day nearly falling against the boulder and hitting her head. Now he knew it was because she was feeling Rebecca die.

"We didn't know."

"You didn't come looking." Her voice rose, and it frightened him.

"Rebecca, tell Grace what you want her to tell others. What do you want her to do? You have to let her go now."

"I could stay here with you," she said, her eyes pleading. "I'll be her."

"Rebecca, I don't love you."

He watched as Grace's eyes grew wide and then closed.

Hurrying to the other side of the drawer, he wrapped his arms around her before she collapsed to the floor.

"Damnit! How does she do that?" Grace clung to his shirt, pulling herself up.

"You remember this time?" he asked.

"I know what it feels like now. I can remember the last time too."

He wanted to scold her for not telling him, but he was just happy she was safe. "She wanted to stay that way."

"I am not giving up my body," she spat the words out directed at Rebecca.

Matthew touched her face. "You're okay? And this is all you, right?"

"Yes. Your grandmother directly asked her to leave me alone."

He couldn't help but smile as he looked into the eyes that now we're so familiar to him.

"Is she gone now?"

"For now. She left a scribbled note in her car for her mother. She didn't think she was going to die, but she wrote it anyway."

"I'll figure out how to mention it."

"Your grandmother says she wants her pink dress, and we're going to let Juan prepare her. She doesn't want to have much more to do with me."

"Okay. I'll tell them I think the pink dress would be nice for her."

Grace turned back to Rebecca and pushed in her drawer.

He wondered if Rebecca had more to say, or if his grandmother was getting an earful.

As Grace closed the door, he felt the pang of sadness replace that anger that had boiled inside him. Rebecca was a constant in his life. He never should have kissed her, and he certainly shouldn't have let her sleep in his bed, but what was done was done. Still, he'd never wished her any harm.

"What are your plans now?" he asked as Grace turned back to him.

"I don't know, I feel as though I should stay around and help."

He didn't like the idea of her being close to Rebecca. Even in death, he didn't know if Rebecca was putting on heirs or not.

"Maybe if you only answered the phone out front."

She chuckled. "Maybe."

"I'm happy to drop you off at home or at your mother's house too."

She cocked her head to the side and narrowed her eyes on him. "I have my car here. Are you afraid that I'll come back if you take me home?"

"I didn't think of it, that's all. I just think I should head over to the Barnes' house and feed them my opinions."

"Last wishes."

"Everyone deserves them, right?" he asked as he looked at the door Rebecca was tucked behind. "I didn't love her."

Grace took his hand and pressed her lips to his knuckles. "I know. And she knows. I felt that lingering even after she left me. Don't feel bad for her, Matthew. If you do, it'll ruin what's to come next."

"What's next, Grace?"

Her lips softened into a smile that melted him in the cold room. "We'll discuss that some other time," she said looking at the wall of drawers. "In some other location. Go to the Barnes'. I'll go find my mother. She'll send me home if she thinks I need to be sent away."

"Maybe you'd better ask your father. He seems to have more insight."

"I'll do just that."

CHAPTER 41

*S*he'd been shunned. Grace wasn't heartbroken about it, but she'd been sent away until Rebecca Barnes' funeral was over, and that would be a few days.

Her mother wouldn't even hear of her setting foot back in the mortuary until then, and her father, who was the one she was trusting most for his decision, said he had to agree. There was too much activity going on for Grace to be safe.

Sitting on her sofa with the romance novel she'd purchased weeks ago resting on her lap, Grace tried to relax. It had been two days since Rebecca had tried to convince Matthew that she could simply assume Grace's body and keep him for herself.

Even in death, Grace wondered how anyone could be so calculating.

In the few days since Rebecca's death, Grace had learned a lot about the woman—and so had Matthew.

He said they'd found the letter she'd written and left in her car. Even though Rebecca had said she was only trying to get attention from attempting suicide, the letter was much darker. He said Rebecca's mother wouldn't go into all of the details, but one of the officers on the case had mentioned that she'd hoped to harm Matthew's relationship and perhaps harm Grace as well.

She supposed Rebecca had done that, though she couldn't imagine she'd planned to do all of that from the other realm.

Then again, Grace couldn't say she understood anything Rebecca Barnes did. Married twice, divorced twice, and still hell bent on making Matthew fall in love with her—that didn't sound like any sane person Grace had even know.

While waiting to be released from what she was deeming purgatory from the dead, she'd done some researching on spirits taking over someone's body and was building herself an arsenal of knowledge so that it would never again happen to her.

One thing was for sure, Rebecca was a strong spirit among the living and the dead. To have manipulated physical items, to have sent so many signals, and to have taken over the body of a living person— even in the spiritual world those were advanced moves—or so she'd read on the internet.

Regardless of what had happened with Rebecca, Grace still felt the same pull to help others finish up what they had left on earth to do. If the time ever came when Nora Campbell continued on, she wasn't sure what she would do. But they'd get to that when the time came.

Grace had also taken it upon herself, while she was home alone for hours on end, to write down all of the things that Matthew had experienced. He'd heard Nora whisper to him, he'd smelled the roses and the earth, and it was him who had chosen the trail to hike when Rebecca was dying. Together, they seemed to have quite a bit of insight into communicating with the deceased.

Matthew had pushed back his piece on the gentlemen in the cemetery until the following week, but she'd seen a glimpse of what Kyle had put together. It was extraordinary. Mrs. Fallon had agreed to a segment too to talk about her cancer support group.

Even Grace's mother had mentioned that Matthew had asked her to appear in one of his segments.

Business went on, even if she was locked away.

Putting down the book, which she'd yet to start, she looked at the clock on the wall. Rebecca's funeral was over two hours ago, and she hadn't heard a word from anyone yet.

Grace knew better than anyone, funerals weren't limited to the service and the burial. There were receptions and more receptions. She hadn't figured to hear from Matthew for a few more hours, but she couldn't help but be anxious about it.

Her mother had told her that the family opted for a private viewing and a closed casket. They both assumed that Rebecca's mother was embarrassed by Rebecca's death. Some people were like that when it came to suicide. Grace had seen it all, and that was most common.

Standing and walking to the kitchen, Grace thought she would take a nice glass of lemonade out to the patio and enjoy the heat that late July offered.

As she sat her glass on the table, the scent of roses lifted up to her. It didn't surround her as it did when Nora was nearby. This was different. Fresh.

When she looked out over her yard, she saw Matthew, shovel in hand, cursing at a rose bush he was planting in her tiny garden.

Joy bubbled in her chest as she leaned out over the railing.

"What are you doing? I thought you were at a funeral."

He looked up at her and wiped the back of his hand over his brow. "Funerals are depressing. Especially that one. I gave my condolences and left as quickly as I could."

"And now what are you doing?"

"Well, come see," he said and flashed her a smile that radiated up to her.

Grace hurried down the steps toward Matthew.

"Grandma wanted you to have a rosebush too." He held out his hand as if to show her the bush. "Now you have your very own Nora Campbell roses."

She felt the tears sting her eyes, and her words jumbled in her throat. For a moment she could only stand and admire the beauty that had been planted in her yard.

"I am truly honored."

"You should be. She thinks the world of you."

That made her giggle. "How do you know that?"

"Because my grandmother was a good judge of character. She chose people to be in her life only if they would matter throughout it. Grace, she chose you in death, and that's a lot longer than life."

Grace pressed her hand to her chest. "Matthew, that was very sweet."

"It's the truth. I talked to my mother about her giving you the bumblebee pin, and she said that they couldn't think of anyone who deserved it more than you. Grace, you might be new to us in the physical sense. Meaning, we just met you. But I come from a long line of wise people, and we know a good person when we meet them."

Now he pulled her close. His face shined from the sweat that beaded on his brow.

"You're a good person, Grace. Perhaps the most kind, gracious, compassionate person I've ever met. I might have needed my grandmother to make our paths cross, but I didn't need her to show me that side of you. You're genuine."

"Matthew," she sighed and could feel the heat of embarrassment rise in her cheeks.

"It's true. I've worried that I tumbled into this relationship with you so quickly that I wasn't thinking. I know you're worried about that too, and that I'm just in mourning and trying to justify it, but that's not true either. In my heart, I know that I truly love you and that it's genuine."

Grace lifted her arms around his neck and gazed into those blue eyes that mesmerized her. "I love you too. And I know it's genuine. We have a lot to learn about each other, but we have time. We have an entire lifetime to learn."

Matthew chuckled. "I guess we have eternity really. Because I know if I pass before you, I'll still be able to talk to you."

Grace rested her cheek against his chest and could hear his heart racing. Love—it was a glorious feeling.

"Grace," he said, and she eased back to look up at him. "I finally figured out my gift from my grandmother. It was to give to you the entire time."

"Your gift?"

"The box that had my name on it. The bumblebee pin was in it, and even after giving it to my mother, she gave it to you."

"It was a very generous gift. One I will cherish the rest of my life."

"I'm glad to hear that." He took her hands and held them. "The other was her wedding veil."

Grace let out a long breath. "She told me about her veil."

Matthew's eyes lit when she said that. "She told you about it."

Rolling her eyes, Grace let out a laugh. "Yes. She told me I could wear it someday, but I thought, even as a spirit, she was crazy."

"She planned it all out. I want you to have the veil, Grace. I want you to wear it."

"And where am I going to wear it?" She continued to laugh as the scent of roses grew even stronger than those on the bush.

"To our wedding."

Now her laughter stopped, and she looked at Matthew whose face was now shroud in seriousness.

"Our wedding?"

He nodded. "I might have a lifetime to learn about you, but I want to do it as your husband. I know, I know, I've only known you a month, but I don't want to spend another day not bound to you forever."

"Oh, Matthew."

"Please don't say no," he begged as he gave her hands a squeeze. "I don't have a ring, but I'll get you one."

"I'm not that shallow. I don't need a ring. I have rosebush and a bumblebee pin. And now I guess I have a veil to wear too," she let out a laugh that masked the tears that were forming.

"So? Will you marry me?" He smiled at her so warmly, it stirred in her belly.

"Under the fireworks on the fourth of July, down by the river."

The smile fell from his lips as he looked down at her. "You're going to make me wait nearly a year?"

Grace smiled up at him as she wrapped her arms around his neck again and pressed a kiss to his lips. "I'm going to make you wait a year to marry me, but I'm going to make you go straight home and pack a bag. Move in with me, Matthew. Give me a year to plan a spectacular wedding, one I can plan with your grandmother, but move in with me and let's start our life together right now."

"My grandmother loved to plan weddings."

"I gathered that when she gave her single grandson her veil."

He laughed as he pressed his forehead to hers. "I will love you through this life and into the next, Grace Carter."

"I'm glad to hear that, Matthew Campbell because I'm the grantor of final goodbyes and I assume that job will last for eternity and I'll need my partner by my side."

ABOUT THE AUTHOR

Bestselling Author Bernadette Marie is known for building families readers want to be part of. Her series The Keller Family has graced bestseller charts since its release in 2011. Since then she has authored and published over thirty-five books. The married mother of five sons promises romances with a Happily Ever After always…and says she can write it because she lives it.

Obsessed with the art of writing and the business of publishing, chronic entrepreneur Bernadette Marie established her own publishing house, 5 Prince Publishing, in 2011 to bring her own work to market as well as offer an opportunity for fresh voices in fiction to find a home as well. Bernadette Marie is also the owner of Illumination Author Events which offers industry education as well as smaller intimate author/reader events.

When not immersed in the writing/publishing world, Bernadette Marie and her husband are shuffling their five hockey playing boys around town to practices and games as well as running their family business of carwash locations. She is a lover of a good stout craft beer and might be slightly addicted to chocolate.

www.ingramcontent.com/pod-product-compliance
Lightning Source LLC
Chambersburg PA
CBHW030644020726
47493CB00006B/1871